Harr Wagner, E. T. Bunyan

The Street and the Flower

A Novel

Harr Wagner, E. T. Bunyan

The Street and the Flower
A Novel

ISBN/EAN: 9783337007522

Printed in Europe, USA, Canada, Australia, Japan

Cover: Foto ©Andreas Hilbeck / pixelio.de

More available books at **www.hansebooks.com**

THE STREET

BY HARR WAGNER
& E. T. BULMAN

FLOWER

THE STREET AND THE FLOWER.

A NOVEL.

BY

HARR WAGNER AND E. T. BUNYAN,

Editors of " The Golden Era."

INTRODUCTORY ESSAY BY

REV. ROBT. MACKENZIE.

A man's misfortunes antedate his birth.

SAN FRANCISCO CAL.
SAN FRANCISCO NEWS COMPANY
1883.

INTRODUCTORY ESSAY.

Some painter enriched our Centennial Exhibition with a picture of the Cæsar on his war-horse. An affrighted woman carrying her child is seen in the distance, escaping for her life; the ruthless hoof of the horse is planted in the bosom of another woman, less fortunate in her escape, while the Cæsar, indifferent to the sufferings of his march, is calmly studying the globe in his hand, planning at what gates he will next marshal his legions, and what country he will next subdue to his scepter.

That proud and ruthless Cæsar is dust to-day; his marchings are all over; his name affrights no woman or child, but his horse goes on, mounted by another and more reckless, cruel, bloodthirsty rider. Cæsar has given place to alcohol; strong drink commands a larger army, besieges and conquers more cities, and tramples into the dust more women and children than ever did the Cæsar.

Women and children are always the victims of the world's passions. Men may have the glory, the fame or the pleasure; women and children have the pains, the privations, the bitter dregs of it all. Man's breast may heave with proud ambition, on the horse; woman's breast is crushed by the cruel hoof. That horse and that rider are making fearful havoc on our own streets. Their victims pass us on every corner in increasing numbers. The mark of the hoof is plainly seen. Their cry is in our ears, and we dare not be deaf to it. It may be true that strong drink and its blighting results have not touched us; but we are surely past the days of the Stoic and the Pharisee who could wrap themselves in their superiority, and thank God they were not as other men. "What is your Christianity to me?" is an accumulating cry coming up from these miserable unfortunates, which we know and feel ought to have a more practical and comprehensive answer. Christian people hear that cry and feel the inadequacy of the work performed. We stand on the corner of some famous streets where these waifs gather in greater numbers, and, looking beyond, we see the spires of our churches that have cost a hundred thousand dollars—costly piles that stand idle and echoless for six days in the week, across whose portals, opened for two hours on the Sunday, few of this class feel welcome, and less come, and we realize that certainly something is wrong. That amount of capital ought not to be locked up at such a small per cent of return.

None feels or regrets this more than the Christian community. There are hundreds who fain would do something, even much, to alleviate and to prevent all this misery, if they only knew what to do and where to do it. Many a willing heart is delayed, waiting for a large opportunity, or discouraged through the failure of an attempt on too grand a scale.

The heroism of books, the chivalric deeds of the past, seem to have all been performed on horseback, by mailed knights who scoured the globe for the relief of the oppressed and the unfortunate. That form of benevolence still lingers in our imagination, and many zealous spirits are idle, waiting the opportunity to come to them, thus grandly and gaily equipped. To-day the world's heroism is not mounted; those that are helping the world along are almost all on foot—humble, unknown and often obscure.

We read in German history how the Northmen came down upon that country, carrying war and ruin with them. Arnulf, a rough but brave man, led his country in the defense. The swampy nature of the ground and the position of the enemy where they were encamped were singularly unfavorable to such fighting as the knightly noblemen had practised before. They were about to retreat, when Arnulf did the most unknightly thing of dismounting, and, taking in his hand the banner of the empire, led the way on foot through the morass to storm the camp. Christian and other philanthropic people must follow Arnulf's example, and go at this work on foot. The benevolence of the world can reach the needy classes in no other way. Let us be willing to do the little things, to speak the simple word, to begin by gathering in and helping the few. Let us be willing to go right into the swamp, as Arnulf did. Our pity will become still more active and practical when it is applied to the prevention of this misery.

"Is she a bad one?" is asked in the following pages. We certainly would discourage nothing done for the redemption of the "bad ones;" but there are thousands of these children who are not "bad ones" yet. They are only on the way—some of them on the verge of it. The painter represents the angels, not lifting the fallen out of the abyss, but drawing back the tempted, persuading them from the leap into it. We will be on the side of the angels when we mass our energies in preventing this misery. In this line many benevolent people are already found reaping rich results. Our kindergartens, our children's sewing schools, our city missions, our mission visitors that go from house to house, are all working in the line of prevention. Impressions of the good are indelibly made upon the hearts of these children that will underlie and outlive all the wounds of the evil they yet may see.

Nor is there any work on earth that so rewards the worker as that which we do for little children. The Saviour is said to have wept three times, and never to have laughed; but surely there was one time in his life when he smiled—when he took the little children in his arms and blessed them—how could he help it? There is something in our ministry to children that opens the widest gates of our own hearts, something which appeals to the very best within us. When the miners of '49 were in our mountains they endured manfully many of the privations of home and family; but it is said when a little child came casually to a camp, they left their work for a time to go and see it, and sometimes gave the proud mother money for the privilege of kissing the little one; it reminded them of home. When Christ was on the earth, the only thing that reminded him of home was little children. We are surely following in worthy footsteps, when by charity or love we gather up one of these little flowers from the merciless street.

ROBERT McKENZIE.

THE ‡ STREET ‡ AND ‡ THE ‡ FLOWER.

PRELUDE.

From out the depths of humanity comes a plaintive cry for help. Myriad voices are combined in the penetrating complaint. This cry, which is voiced by tears, has been uttered by every human being. With some it has been the cry for bread, some for clothes, some for friends, some for freedom, some for genius, and with others for recognition. Plato heard the cry of humanity for help; he gave the people philosophy. Luther heard the wail; he reformed religion. Dickens saw the tears of poverty in the streets of London; he planted flowers there and made poverty eminently respectable. Our Pilgrim Fathers heard the cry, and freedom lived. John Brown heard the faint echo of the negro's plaintive song, and we are doubly free. The cry for help has reached above mortal ears, and a favorable answer is found in the gradual progression of the race. But life is a web. There are few weavers and much material. That part of the web which is limited by the confines of this city comprises the action and philosophy of this story. The weavers are those who have listened to humanity's cry. Some have listened to the whispers of an angel—a bad angel. Some of the weavers tangle the already tangled web, and ruin the material. It is our intention to discriminate closely between the true and false position of social reformers; to give the true principles of social

ethics; to ridicule some and to praise others who now figure
prominently in social affairs.   Poverty and love—for love, not
sentimentality, is the mainspring of every emotion—wealth and
philosophy—for philosophy governs the proper distribution of
all wealth—are the accompaniments of the story.   The prelude
now ends.   The story begins.

CHAPTER I.

"Heaven is not far removed in our infancy."

In the chill, gloom and squalor of one of the dingiest houses of Benton Park a child caught the breath of heaven, and Miff had a motherless sister.

The bright-eyed boy, ragged, healthy, immoral and dirty, touched with his finger tips the cold, purple lips of his mother, whose life ended when his sister's began.

Six years previous to a time, it matters little when, Miff was born into this straggling world. His misfortunes antedated his birth. Jared Renwood, his father, was a man whose posterity claim no honor through inherited qualities. He was in his earliest youth crushed and warped out of all manly shape and characteristics. Life to him was a mere song, not a song of home, but of the concert hall, low, lewd and inharmonious. Touch him gently with the sharp pencil of truth. Let the fog of the city mantle his weaknesses. He is a man, a father—the paragon of animals and the wonder of society. The bloated face calls for a woman's kind toilet powder; his nose need be painted with the hue of a rose—a white rose; the eyes in the elbow of his coat sleeve need be patched with silver lining; paint him no blacker than he is, or by the darkness of Erebus, a paint blacker than crime will have to be discovered.

What right had Jared Renwood to have born into this world a child tainted with bad blood, albeit a spice of nobleness came from a gentle mother, and the germ of a soul was caught in the first breath as it fluttered and fell from the edge of a cloud to the soulless earth. The world wants more gods.

There was a presiding deity of creation; now let us have a presiding deity of procreation. If there had been some one to see that all were born right, Miff's career would have been like the vast majority —unwritten.

The family of Renwoods, who lived in Benton Park, consisted of Jared Renwood, his wife and boy Miff. But in a day the family was changed. Mrs. Renwood, a kind, gentle and refined woman, was buried. Jared Renwood was dead—drunk, and the infant child was kindly cared for by Mrs. Martin, a good motherly soul, who had only ten children of her own to care for and hard bone labor to support them. Jared Renwood made his home in the saloons. Miff took care of himself, picking up a lesson here and there on the ways of the world, fighting this and stealing that, until a year had passed, bringing a sort of reliant, defiant and immature manhood to the sorry denizen of the street. A hallowed affection existed between him and his baby sister. Every day he would run across the street and touch her soft cheek, pinch her hand and pull out the longest delicate hair he could find on the bald, peach-shaped head. When there was an expressionless smile there was a little more sunshine for him. His affection was the pure, natural, kindred love.

One day, Mrs. Martin called Miff over and asked him what he would call his sister.

" Baby, to be sure," he answered.

" No, that won't do; you must give her some nice lady's name."

" Call her somethin' that'll make her good," said Miff.

" Let us call her Bona—that means good," said Mrs. Martin.

And Miff was satisfied, and as he called his little sister Bona for the first time, he baptized her with a kiss, and was happy in having a sister with such a splendid name.

In the city, at this time, was a noble, self-sacrificing woman who was looking after homeless and motherless children. A system of schools, called children's gardens, was established, and into these kindergartens were gathered many a child who received such moral and religious instructions that their after lives were made a satisfaction to themselves and a glory and honor to humanity. Mrs. Kate Benson was at the head of this work; she perfected the plans, and, by her own personality, overcame much of the prejudice that existed against all practical work in the way of reform.

Benton Park knew Mrs. Benson. Once she had taken a motherless child from the place, and had given it a home. Mrs. Martin would willingly have kept Bona, but alas, poverty forbade, as it has often, before and since, a generous impulse.

Renwood was not consulted. He never contributed a cent toward the child's support, and did not even give a father's love.

Mrs. Benson, on learning the history of Bona, gladly accepted the protegée. Alas for poor Miff, when he returned, Bona was not to be seen.

"Where is Bona?" was his first inquiry. When told a good woman had come for his sister, he insisted that a bad woman, a wicked woman, had taken his Bona.

When Jared Renwood learned that his little daughter had been taken charge of by a charitable lady, he began to curse the women in general, who were always bothering poor folks under the guise of charity, yet their main object was to get a man into church, in order to get collections from him. He took Miff by the hand, and together they went to the corner saloon, and there, in the crowd of half-drunken loafers, he told his tale of woe, and heard the words of sympathy expressed by those present.

Miff's hands twitched. His eyes flashed, and, looking up defiantly, he said: "I am going to get my sister back. The bad woman"—and tears choked his utterance. The bar-maid gave him a glass of beer to drink. The loafers cheered him and called him a little man, and petted his tendency to their own fallen estate. In this corner saloon—call it a grocery store; dignify it by any name you please; call it a Crystal Palace, Saints' Rest, Sinners' Retreat, Palace Grocery Store, The Elite; call it Paradise, if you choose—the fact remains that no name will ever remove the evil it has done nor lessen the influence in destroying the children who frequent the place to perform a mother's errand.

Miff grew up in the company of his father, who liked him because he was a lovable child—a mixture of the good and bad, a boy with a capacity for good, but trained to evil. A tender and refined mother had guarded his existence until he was six years of age; then a father's evil associates and a father's bad example influenced him. Miff was of the street; upon the highway he lived, and the alleys were his retreat. He had a home— a cold, comfortless home. The sunshine and the companionship of the street were dearer to him than his cheerless room. Almost every day he would inquire of Mrs. Martin for Bona, and his grief did not lessen with time. The little sister had made an impression upon his childish heart.

One day he was playing in the sand on one of the hills back of Benton Park, where he met a little girl about his own age. They pulled up the weeds and tossed the sand into each other's eyes, and Miff, to give his mate a fair advantage, threw against the sea breeze. At last, becoming tired of the sport, he said to her abruptly:

"What is your name?"

Not waiting for an answer, he pulled her down on the sand by his side and told her about the wicked charity woman who took his sister Bona. It was a pitiful story, and every time he told it the sadness became more marked.

While they were talking, a policeman approached them.

"That is a charity man," said the little girl. "He took my brother for takin' something from Shinlers."

At this information the little couple started for Benton Park. When near the place, Miff again asked the girl her name, and learned that she was called Viola.

They found a man waiting at Mrs. Martin's for their return. As soon as they arrived, Mrs. Martin told Miff that a real nice old man wanted him to go with him and grow up to be a fine man, so that when he would find his sister she would be proud of having such a nice brother. The information startled Miff.

"Is he a charity man?" And, not waiting for an answer, he fled from the room and ran down the street toward the corner saloon. "It's a charity man after me!" he yelled back to Viola, as he saw her running after him at a speed nearly as rapid as his own.

CHAPTER II.

" The children figure in the giant mass
    Of things to come."

Down the street Miff and Viola ran, their speed diminishing with their fear. They halted at last in front of a dwelling, on which the sign "For Rent" had been obscured by the corroding influence of time. They stood, hesitated a moment; then Miff, taking Viola by the hand, crept through a narrow opening in the fence, and, going to the rear of the house, they looked for a hiding-place. A basement door was open. Trembling with excitement, and believing that the charity man was close behind, determined to catch them, the couple fearlessly entered where women would not dare to tread. The dampness of the cellar, the darkness, and now and then the move of some harmless insect, perhaps the fluttering of a bat, made it decidedly disagreeable for so young a twain. They crept into a corner, and economized as much space as possible. His shoulder touched hers, cheek caressed cheek, eye confided in eye. The trust and confidence of a woman will make the most arrant coward valorous, and Viola, by some freak of human nature, trusted her little companion, Miff.

The darkness of night coming over the city did not change the light of their hiding-place. The fog at sunrise was not even noticed by them. They slept on. Viola awoke. Miff was sleeping still. His fingers were entwined in her hair. One hand was in his pocket. His body curled up like a ball. Viola rubbed her eyes with a doubled fist, and then, looking fondly a moment at Miff, leaned over and kissed him. He uttered the word " mother," and opened his eyes. The kiss to him was a mother's benediction. He was no doubt transferred to Paradise—the happy land of dreams. Viola's kiss made the dream of his mother real in the awakening moment, but it dispelled the illusion, and the transportation from dreamland left him, as it does all, in a cold and uncharitable world. When he was wide awake he told Viola that his mother had come back, and that just before he awoke she had kissed him.

" Did she ? why, I did too," said Viola.

" And she put my hair back this way," continued Miff, as he stroked his hair.

" That's what I was doing, too."

A quizzical look came into Miff's face. He did not quite understand a mother's kiss, and could not remember that Viola kissed him.

" I am awful hungry," pleaded Viola.

Miff took some sassafras and some browned coffee, which he had supplied himself with from the counter of the corner saloon —where it is generally kept to purify the breath after polluting the throat with bad whiskey—from his pocket, and soon they were enjoying their frugal meal. The breakfast was suddenly interrupted by slow, measured sounds on the stairs. It was the measured sound of step after step, the somewhat sharper sound of a cane, as it did its master's service descending the stairs. The children were frightened. They huddled together, and Viola whispered: " What will we do?" The sound came nearer. The last step seemed to be reached. Miff placed Viola in a corner, and taking a board placed it in front of her, and then stood guard. He saw a door opening. The form of a man approaching. His voice trembling too much to do him service, yet ready to protect his companion, he cried out:

" Viola is not here!"

"And who are you, my little man?" was spoken in a kindly voice.

Miff was afraid, though—a kind voice is as full of treachery to a child as to a man, at times. He stood against the board so hard that a sob was heard, and a plaintive "Don't" from Viola.

"Come, my little fellow, why did you come here and who is that behind the board?"

The questioner was Oswald Grayson, a peculiar man. His features were no index to his character. A huge lump deformed his back. His head was large while his limbs were diminutive; in fact, his body was so out of proportion that he was compelled to reverse the common process of putting on a shirt. His form was abnormal—too ill-shaped to be agreeable, and not enough to arouse active pity. He was not poor, neither was he rich; for wealth is measured by health, and personal property is worth a world if it consists in a handsome face and form. Oswald Grayson lived alone. The neighbors knew him only to shun him, and the street knew him not. The old house was his abiding place. He was as sensitive as the plant that withers at a touch, and the world was to him no more than an unheard of country is to us. The house that everybody supposed was unoccupied was Oswald Grayson's home.

Miff did not answer his inquiry, but Viola, with the keen perception of her nature, stepped from behind the board and said:

"It's me." She recognized kindness in the voice, and dreaded not the man's presence. Seeing him, excited her pity, while it aroused Miff's fears.

Mr Grayson took the children, Miff reluctantly, Viola willingly, up the stairs, and gave them a bountiful supply of his own breakfast. They ate heartily, although they believed they were the guests of a veritable ghost. Rumor said the old house was haunted, and surely the presence of Grayson gave credence to the story. **Mr.** Grayson **went over to Viola,** and, taking her on his knee, began to talk **to her.** Soon they were engaged in an interesting conversation. Miff eyed them suspiciously.

"And so your name is Viola, and you live at Benton Park. Now, **won't** you tell me your other name?"

"It **is** Viola Proctor."

At the mention of the name, the color left the old man's face, and a deep, harsh and unnatural look overspread his countenance. He rudely pushed Viola from his knee, and muttered unintelligible invectives. "I knew it; the face was like hers—as winning, as lovable, **and in her** willingness to follow **me** and to be with **me, I can** trace her mother's nature. **A nature** willing but weak, **strong to attract,** but repelling **every attention that did not** gratify **her vanity."** Going to an old stand, he unfolded a package of **letters,** and **took out a withered** violet. **The children** watched him, for his movements were strange, and his agitation perceptible even to them.

He held the violet in his hand, and, raising it on a level with his eyes, fixed his gaze upon it. "Oh, that my affection could wither like the violet, and that remembrance would fade like its color! The years of the past rise before me. I **see** again **and live over the scenes** of twenty years ago. The vision **of a** beautiful woman rises before me as if to mock my deformity. I smile and she smiles in return. I love and she loves **in return;** but alas, the sacrifice was too great for her, and those letters, yellowed with age, and this faded violet, are all that linger of a lingering affection. **Viola Proctor—and the violet.** Did Edna remember the flowers, and **did** she **christen her** child—come Viola." **And** he took **the** little girl in his arms **and** kissed her tenderly.

Miff, ever restless, **took** Viola by the hand as soon as Mr. Grayson put her **down,** and drew her towards the door, but Mr. Grayson did not let them go until he had won their childish confidence and friendship by several gifts. Viola carried with her a bunch of violets.

The children returned to Benton Park. The charity man was no longer there, unfortunately for Miff. The children's absence from Benton Park was not commented upon. A drunken father asked:

"Where's my boy to-night?" and went on drinking; and Edna Proctor knew not, and neither did she care, of the where-abouts of Viola. A hard fate had crushed out a mother's affec-tion. The world and life among the low had dulled her sensibil-ities until she was worse than a brute, because the instincts of the animal are never debased. She stood behind a bar on Bar-bary Coast.

From the first night with Mr. Grayson, Miff and Viola prowled the streets as chums. Their condition was to be in an unwashed, forlorn, uncared-for and hungry state. They wandered about the dirty streets, picking up a living as best they could. They grew in years and ignorance, and were worthy members of the hoodlum society, in which organization they were elected honor-ary members for life, or as long as their good behavior continued. The street was their home; their mode of living precarious. The necessities of life made them necessarily bad. If sent for beer, they would stop to taste, to sip. Their lives were in the same channel, though for weeks they were separated. Viola was with her mother some, and Miff kept up a speaking acquaintance with his father.

Our castaway, Viola, for she was no better, attracted one day by a little bit of color while sprawling in the back yard with some other children, inhaled the fragrance of a violet. Unconsciously she watched it. The other children had a monopoly of the play, so they did not disturb her. She fell asleep by its side and dreamed, perhaps, of bright flowers, graceful forms and a paradise more beautiful than ever her fancy pictured. She transplanted the violet into a mug, and placed it in her mother's dismal room. She clasped her hands in joy when she saw it was growing and continuing to bloom more and more beautiful. She wondered and wondered, and unconsciously exercised the innate sense of worship of the beautiful, which is implanted in every human heart, and causes the merest babes to rejoice at the light and shapes, the color and proportion of all objects, and to be entranced by the harmony of sound. Viola loved the flower passionately. Her infatuation was noticed. Perhaps she rejoiced in the color and light of the flower, because she listened not to the harmony of a mother's lullaby. A nature has capacities; ambition satisfies the love of the soul, instead of the diviner love of woman. Man loves woman less because he loves success more, and woman loves man more because she loves success less. Thus it was with the child. She loved the violet more because she loved her mother less.

One day, when watering the flower with water she carried in the hollow of her little hand, her mother passed by, and, seeing her, knocked the mug from the stand, crushing the stem and destroying her flower. The grief of Viola was intense. She gave her mother a bewildered, sad, yet passionate look. Picking up the flower, she put it in the bosom of her old, faded dress. She carried it for days concealed thus, and when the flower bore no resemblance to its former beauty she cried most piteously. But, alas, it was not only the violet that was crushed, but Viola was trodden down. Every good motive, every noble impulse, was crushed as was the violet in its infancy. Viola is the flower of the street. She was planted there; watered in early childhood by the goodness of God; but no flower can grow and blossom and make fragrant the air, that is left uncared for in the street.

Her mother sent her to the corner to buy some fruit, and ordered her to take, when no one was looking, some peaches. This was her first lesson in practical morality. Her success made her bold, and when she wanted anything there was no commandment to bother her conscience.

Miff and Viola would wander on the street for days at a time, watching eagerly for opportunities to secure anything by stealth or sharpness. They became experts, professionals. They were found out, of course; but every one seemed to be aware of their helpless condition, and let them off with a rap over the head or a twist of the ear.

Miff's practical lesson on morals one day was never forgotten by her.

A few weeks after they had become professionals, Miff observed Viola sitting on the pavement near a fruit stand, and set himself to watch. Viola shifted her position occasionally, getting nearer and nearer, until she was quite close to the stand. Soon one hand reached out and brought back a paper of grapes; then another attempt was made; then her position was slowly shifted until she was behind the corner again. Miff laughed heartily, but looked serious as he saw Viola running at full speed down the street. He started after her on a run. She heard his footsteps, and, thinking a policeman was after her, increased her pace. A race began. Round corners, through alleys, up and down streets. As they were running up Pacific street, Viola threw down the grapes. Miff stopped, picked them up, and began feasting. Viola looked around, and saw Miff with the grapes. She came back panting, but smiling.

"Oh, Miff," cried Viola, "I thought somebody was after me."

Then Miff told her that it was the very worst policy to run, after taking anything, when no one was looking.

He passed over the bag of grapes to her, and gave her a peach that he had pocketed a few moments before.

They returned together to Benton Park, talking over their prospects for the morrow. The minutes—light to some, heavy to some, leaving in their track woe and joy; golden minutes, leaden minutes; for some happiness, for others grief—flew by. The life of Miff and Viola is a question for the wisest philosophers of social problems to settle. The theory of their lives and reformation, the school boy's philosophy is adequate to such a demand. But, looking at them from every aspect, taking into consideration their moral and physical faculties—and souls to be saved, who can kindle a blaze from such hard flint, and make practical a theory for the development of the hoodlum element in society?

What resemblance do Miff and Viola bear to that poetical image which declares man to be noble in reason, infinite in faculty, express and admirable in form and bearing, like an angel in action, like a god in apprehension, the beauty of the world, the paragon of animals? It is best for us not to examine too curiously, for there is shame to the human race in the lives of Miff and Viola, the street and the flower. The redeeming feature is found in Bona, who will walk through our next chapter, making it radiant with her presence.

CHAPTER III.

"No mother who stands on low ground herself can hope to place her children on a loftier plane. They may reach it, but it will not be through her."

Mrs. Kate Benson was a lovable woman. We call her a lovable woman because all women are not lovable. Indeed, we consider them a rarity. A sweet temper, a kind disposition, a philanthropy that embodied the world's friendliness, and a mind that recognized all creeds, were her prominent characteristics. She founded a home for little girls, and in this home Bona was placed. Each year, from the slums of the city, she would gather three infants, and take them under her care; and the recognition seemed to come to her in this world, for, while her hair is slightly tinged with gray, she is still young enough to appreciate the gratitude of her matured protegées. Ingratitude may be a prominent trait of human character, but future years will have to change our present opinion before we accuse humanity of such an ignoble part.

Bona was dearly loved by Mrs. Benson, and "Mother" lisped Bona, as soon as she could speak. Mrs. Benson placed her in a Kindergarten school, and there, under the excellent influence of such a praiseworthy system of teaching, and the careful training, Bona grew in years and beauty. At the age of ten, she joined the Flower Mission Society, and took a great delight in charitable work. One day, while on her way to the jail, she saw a queer couple on the street. A ragged boy of seventeen and a girl a few years younger—hoodlums, yes, veritable vagabonds. Legitimate children of San Francisco's low-ebb society.

The boy's trousers were **tattered** at the edges—were old, patched, torn, and large enough for two such boys. The girl was attired in a new calico, and she all the while was turning half around as if **to see if** it fit her on the back. The dress was **a present to** her from Oswald Grayson, the hermit of the haunted house. Some years have passed since we saw them before, yet we recognize in the hoodlums Miff and Viola. Miff stopped and looked at Bona, stared **at her,** and, taking a bunch of her flowers, buried his face among the buds and blossoms, as if to get the sweetest perfume. Viola, Miff's constant companion and frequently his imitator, grabbed another bunch and did likewise.

Bona looked at them in **astonishment.**

"**Give me my** flowers," she said, kindly.

"Won't you **buy a bouquet, please, from a** poor orphan boy?" said Miff, as he offered Bona one of the stolen bunches.

Viola laughed heartily as Bona handed him the required dime.

"Buy mine, too; I want something to eat." And she threw such a hungry look in her eyes, and in her voice such a woeful tone, that Bona made the second purchase, and was a₃ well off in her bargain as most people who buy from beggars.

The **two** hoodlums **were** not satisfied with their bargain. They wanted more, **and** Miff, understanding the power of flattery, said: "You're a nice little girl. Won't you give us somethin' towards gettin' a pair of shoes?" **He** looked dolefully at his feet, and thrust his toes **in such a way as to** make the holes in the leather very conspicuous.

In reply, Bona drew from her pocket a ticket **of** invitation **to** the children's prayer meeting on Pacific street, and handed it to him. Viola, thinking it a ticket for charity, held **out** her hand for one. Miff gave a peculiar whistle when he saw the nature **of** the card. He could not read, **yet had** learned to spell before his mother died, and frequently amused himself by spelling words on signs. By his clan he was considered a highly-educated gentleman. Viola trusted all to his great wisdom and learning. Their heads were very close together, as Miff slowly spelt and pronounced: "Admit the bearer to children's prayer meeting and supper."

"Prayer meeting and supper. Say, can we have the supper without the prayer meeting?"

The two hoodlums laughed so heartily that Bona started on a run. Miff, with no evil intentions whatever, darted after her at full speed, and Viola kept up in the rear. A heavy hand was placed on Miff's shoulder, and Viola darted around a corner. Bona ran on.

"Here, sir."

"I did not mean any harm, sir. I was only trying to catch her to give them back," said Miff, as he held to view the supper and prayer meeting tickets. The tall form of Dr. Halstead towered over Miff; the sharp eyes assumed a stern look, and made him tremble with fear.

Bona saw Miff in the hands of Dr. Halstead, and, forgetting her fear, stopped and returned.

"Please, sir," she said, "let him go. He did not mean to hurt me."

"No, miss; I only wanted to thank you for those tickets, and for buying my bouquets." And the fellow blushed with shame as he remembered the bouquets.

Dr. Halstead, amused at the turn affairs had taken, still held to the hoodlum. "I think, sir, I will put you in the House of Correction."

"Oh, don't, sir. I have been there [three times, and was beaten nearly dead."

"What do you do for a living?"

"We sell flowers. We do anything. Viola scrubs sometimes, and I watch places for people. We are not vagabonds."

The sympathies of Bona were now fully aroused, and she said again:

"Please let him go."

Dr. Halstead took from his pocket a half dollar, and gave it to Miff, and invited him to visit his night school, and fit himself to be a man. Bona's plea was effective, and Miff started off to hunt his almost inseparable companion, Viola, but not until Bona's little hand rested in his. A look, a steady gaze, and an indescribable something passed between them—not recognition, but the first impulse of an affinity that governs the likes and dislikes of all the relations of life.

"Indiscriminate charity again," said Dr. Halstead, as he walked down the street, musing on the incident. "I wonder if in giving that worthless fellow a half dollar I have not assisted in making a criminal. Charity, after all, is a reward for crime, and indiscriminate charity would make beggars of us all, and beggary is only a step from crime. An honest beggar is like an honest thief."

"Well, you should get out of my way," said Dr. Halstead, as he almost stumbled over a small girl on the street.

"I'm hurt," piteously cried the girl, and two big tears glistened in her eyes, which she tried to make as conspicuous as possible by having them run down the groove in her face.

Dr. Halstead looked at her kindly. Kindness always reaps its own reward, for Viola began: "Mamma sent me out to buy some bread, and I lost the money here." And she made a diligent search, but of course could not find that which she had not lost. But she succeeded in bringing some tears to the surface, and with an unnatural boo-hoo the sympathies of Dr. Halstead were again aroused, and, taking from his pocket a fifty-cent piece, gave it to Viola, who looked up, thanked him, and then made away as rapidly as possible, for she could hardly keep back the gleam of satisfaction.

"Hello, we're in luck to-day—a dollar and twenty cents and two prayer meeting tickets. Enough to live on a week," said Miff. "That was a good job we put up on the old man. He is a regular sympathizer, ain't he? I told you if you would hurry and play the game, you'd make something."

Dr. Halstead walked a few steps; then turned and looked in the direction Viola had taken.

"I wonder," he thought, "if that was indiscriminate charity again. Well, the poor girl is welcome to it. I only wish that there was more individual charity."

He walked on down until he reached Pacific street, and there, under the shadow of the sign "Children's Home," he entered. The faces of a score of children were brightened by his presence. He was in his own home, built by his money, for the purpose of training children of the street in useful employments. They were gathered from the streets and from the hovels of the poor. The low, the vile—ay, the worst of mankind—were gathered here; but a week had a wonderful influence on their lives. A week of good food, good lodgings and kindness made them new creatures. As he looked upon their busy fingers, or listened to their lessons, no conscience accused him of mistaken charity. A consciousness of noble work of reformation, of the rescuing of lives from shame and degradation, came to him as he studied his work.

Dr. Halstead, the charity man—for it was he who endeavored to place Miff, years ago, under good influence, away from the influence of the street, of parental crime, the crime of a bad example—was a reformer, an ideal reformer; not a blatant talker, but a doer. He was every inch a man; measure as you

will, the dimensions of a square man will always be found.   His
face was beautiful—not with the lines of beauty, but with the
furrows of care.   His tall form was slightly stooped—curved,
not by dissipation, but by burdens of an active life.   There are
a great many people born in the world who are not wanted.
They are like a standing army in time of peace—no earthly
good.   The world, they say, owes them a living.   They generally get it through prison bars.

Dr. Halstead was not a man of this type.   He was a man of
large wealth, and with a liberal spirit as broad as humanity.
Poverty to some is a load, and wealth is a load to others.   Thus
it is that we can bear each other's burdens.   Dr. Halstead endeavored not to lift the burden of poverty so much as the burden of evil and vitiated habit, and his charity did not begin at
home, but at the spring-time of life.   Charity should begin
with the rising generation.   The old are past redemption.

Mrs. Benson waited a long while for the return of Bona;   the
darling girl was her favorite.   There was nothing of a past life
clinging to her.   The ten years in a Kindergarten and excellent
home training had made her fine in thoughts, graceful in action
and polite in manners.   The day passed, and no Bona came.   A
week of fruitless search, but no Bona.   Then the following advertisement appeared in the "Chronicle":

LOST—A child ten years of age; small for her age; dark hair; full, round,
expressive brown eyes; fair complexion; wore a small ring on her finger, en-
graved Kindergarten; a dark gingham dress; when last seen was on her way
to the jail with some flowers.   Any information will be thankfully received
by Mrs. Benson, Van Ness Avenue.

Dr. Halstead, noticing the advertisement, sent Mrs. Benson a
note informing her of the incident that happened on the morning
Bona was missed.   A search was made for Miff.   When found,
and told the mission of the inquiries, he assumed a knowing

manner and refused to give any information until rewarded. He recognized the sympathizer in Dr. Halstead.

" I'll tell you all about it for five dollars."

He got his five dollars.

" I was going up Montgomery street one morning, and met a little girl about ten years of age. She was carrying a lot of flowers. I bought some from her and then sold them back again. She gave me a dime and then ran off. That's all I know."

A dissatisfied look went around, and Dr. Halstead and Mrs. Benson knew that Miff had legally swindled them out of five dollars.

A few moments afterward Miff met the soiled flower of the street, Viola.

" I made a big stake; look here," as he held up the five dollar gold piece. " I'll soon go into the wholesale swindling business, if I keep on doing so well," said Miff.

" I am so glad, because you will take me to the theatre to-night."

" I am real sorry the little girl is lost, though."

" Say," says Miff, " I wonder if you couldn't make something out of them, too."

" I'll try."

" Yes, but wait a few days. Let us go home now."

Down the street to an unfrequented portion of the city they go. In an old house, weather-beaten and decayed, standing on a square and houses around a disgrace to any city. A saloon is in the basement. The young hoodlums go up the stairs laden with dirt and reach a cheerless room. An old straw mattress serves as a bed. A chair, a stool, a broken mirror, a tin basin, a mattress and a violet in bloom are all that are in the room.

Ever since Oswald Grayson had called Viola a violet, and since the time the violet was crushed by her mother's willful hand, she had cherished a fond, childish affection for the violet. They ate a hearty supper, and, agreeing to go to the theatre on the next night, they went to sleep. They were lovers, but they knew not sentiment. They were partners.

Like doves they were mated, but their cooing we do not understand. They were ignorant of morals and religion. It is necessary to state this that you judge them not harshly, and look upon them with an uncharitable spirit. They slept on. The stars shone through the roof overhead—the eyes of God watching his children. Neither Miff nor Viola had ever looked reverently toward the sky. They never said a prayer. The great world moves on. Mighty men of science prove remarkable things, but Miff and Viola, unconscious of all, grow deeper and deeper in ignorance and crime.

CHAPTER IV.

"We each furnish to an angel who stands in the sun a single observation."

Ignorance sleeps late in the morning. Crime hides its sinister face from the rays of the rising sun. The honest laborer had earned a loaf of bread by the sweat of his brow before Miff and Viola were aroused from their slumbers.

"Come," said Miff, "let us get some breakfast."

Viola lazily gazed for a moment through the portals of the roof, then turned, as if to take another nap.

"Come," and Miff roughly assisted her to rise.

"Where will we go for breakfast, this morning?" asked Viola.

"Let us go up town and eat with the other people," replied Miff.

"Well, we are rich now, and can feast the same as other folks."

They turned the corner at Montgomery and started up town. They passed a window ornamented with tempting viands, but a gruff waiter standing at the entrance bid them go on. The next place they quietly sneaked in, and sought the most hidden corner. Their inferiority was felt, painfully realized, when the better trained rudely stared at the hoodlums, who quailed beneath the gaze of the reputed polite. The waiter espied them shortly, and, instead of taking their order, gave them one to leave directly.

"It's mean that won't let us eat anywhere," said Miff.

Again they tried, where hundreds were being fed, but none so disconsolate and forlorn as Miff and Viola. They quietly pushed open the door and took a seat as near the exit as possible.

Miff, wiser than many a graduate, took from his pocket the five-dollar coin and placed it in a conspicuous place near his plate. When the waiter, who happened to be one of the proprietors, saw the gold piece, he changed his half-formed plan to order them out, and bid them take a seat in a corner.

Miff gave Viola the bill of fare, but it had no meaning to her. She could not read. Miff managed to spell out the articles of diet that he wanted—a half spring chicken, tom-cods, a sirloin steak, potatoes, hot cakes, chocolate and a dozen other edibles. The waiter stared in amazement, and if a sight of the golden coin had not convinced him that the check would be cashed, Miff and Viola would not have had their order filled. Thus it is that money wins. If you give a man money, you give him the homage of the world. Money conquers and rules with a despotic power. Independence is greater than money, but without money there is no independence. The sight of a five-dollar coin enabled Miff and Viola to secure a breakfast at a fashionable restaurant, and a flashing diamond on the shirt bosom of a debased man will win a smile from the proudest lady in the land.

The two hungry hoodlums enjoyed their feast immensely. Miff paid the bill with the air of a millionaire, and, taking Viola by the arm, the twain walked away from the restaurant, having partaken of the heartiest meal of their lives. On their way back to their home—what a fine word to describe these quarters—Miff could not restrain his propensity to increase his material wealth, and lessen considerably his standing in the community, by taking on the sly anything that was not watched. They passed by a baker's wagon, and inside were some fine loaves of bread. Miff approached the wagon, crept to the open door, and returned with some bread and several pies under his coat. Viola imitated his action. A policeman saw her, and in a moment the club— the wonderful club, the useless club, the club of the policeman, a relic of Roman barbarism—was raised above Miff's head, while the bread and pies fell to the pavement, the visible evidence of guilt. The gruff policeman—there are no kind policemen in this city—arrested them in the name of justice, and led the trembling pair to jail. In the afternoon the Police Court was to be graced by their presence.

" They have us at last."

" It is all my fault, too," said Viola.

" Well, never mind," replied Miff; " we will be more careful in the future." And, going over to her, stooped and kissed her, and then turned away.

" Come back," said Viola. And, as he turned, she threw her arms about his neck and kissed him again and again.

The jailer passing, halted, and opening the cell, ordered Viola to follow. The two were separated.

Do you suppose that they should express sorrow for their petty crime? Perhaps you believe in the motto, " Train up a child in the way it should go, and when it is old it will not depart therefrom." If so, is it not equally true, "Train up a child in the way it should not go, and when it is old it will not depart therefrom."

The lessons of life were learned in the street. A slice of bread and butter were more to them than all the virtues, the exercise of which bestows the light of eternal happiness. Why, from very necessity, they believed that bad was good. It is one of the awful mysteries of the times how they were allowed to grow up in ignorance and crime. If there be truth in the newspaper columns, humanity is in sympathy with them as a class whom it is man's duty to lift from the dust. Yet who dare say that Miff and Viola were not fared to be dead to the knowledge of virtue, to earn the condemnation of men and to offend the goodness of the Supreme.

A smile of recognition—a sad, sorrowful smile—passed from Miff to Viola as they met in the afternoon in the Police Court. A few hoodlums and the policeman testified, and Miff confessed his crime of stealing, and Viola was too much frightened to speak.

"Three months in the House of Correction," spoke the Police Court Judge.

Miff and Viola were hurried away, and for three months they disappear from really active life.

The next case called was that of a man for beating his wife and neglecting his children. A dozen neighbors testified to his cruel neglect of an idiotic child and of his neglect of the others. His wife was put on the stand, bearing the marks of hard blows. The man did not deny that he beat her. The neighbors say cruelly; blood stains were on the floor. No aggravation on the wife was put in evidence. A clear case of base cruelty. A heavy fine was imposed, oh no—a few days imprisonment was all. Compare the two unequal sentences and you have the vulgar value put on bread and pies, and the value of human flesh in the Police Court market.

A group of reformers, mostly women, met at the Children's Home in order to consider the various reforms. There was a tall, angular woman, who cared not for helpless children, who, like the judge, would pass an unjust sentence on incorrigible children, but at the same time be lenient with the parent who forces such children upon the State.

Society in this city is built from the social ruin of two generations. It needs a revolution—a declaration of independence to be free, not from one, but from a thousand shams. Pretension and sham, sham and pretension, and intensified shams, are the visible mainstays of society. You hear more said in praise of an elegant dancer than a brilliant conversationalist. Mrs. A. Devine, the reformer of skirts, is more widely known than Dr. Halstead, the indiscriminate charity man. Yet, the Children's Home was built by the latter's money. If the treasurer of any benevolent association found out that he gave money to any charity, not through a committee, he was censured by all.

Mrs. Devine rose first among the reformers, and said: "The most important movement of this age is the advancement of social science. Women must have the ballot, and must reform their dress, habits and manners. Men do not sympathize with women in this, but we should have their aid and support."

"I should think," said Dr. Halstead, "that it is more important for men to sympathize with the helpless children—to reform Barbary Coast, rather than Nob Hill. I met, but a day or two ago, two children raised among the saloons and dens of vice. They were an incumbrance to society, blots, waifs, and will furnish countless themes and oceans of words to reformers. To-day I read that they have been sentenced to the House of Correction. Yesterday I met a homeless girl on the streets. I asked a policeman to give her lodgings in the jail or station house over night. He asked me, 'Is she a bad one.' A good girl, homeless, friendless and hungry, must qualify herself by crime before she secures a refuge from the city. Let the policeman cry, 'Move on." We must give the unfortunates work, and in this building we must organize a sewing school."

Thus it was with Dr. Halstead—ever opposed to the lip philanthrophy that invariably closes the pockets, he was eminently practical, and indiscriminate charity did not worry him. If he saw a hungry boy on the street, he did not wish to secure a committee of experts to examine his appetite, but his hand was in his pocket.

Then Mrs. Benson said: "I was passing down Market street yesterday afternoon. Two fashionable young men passed by a poor blind boy, who stood by a lamp post with his hand appealingly held forth. One of the young men struck the hand a blow with his cane. The other laughed at the joke and fright of the poor boy. Dr. Halstead came up a moment afterwards and gave the poor boy money. The policeman, noticing the adventure, bid the blind boy move on. The young men—or rather, matured brutes—were smiled on, while the unfortunate boy felt his way cautiously to another square. I claim, that after all, Dr. Halstead's method was the true *modus operandi* of charity. Reform schools have a purpose. Free kindergartens for homeless children do a good work. The Old Ladies' Home will supply a long-felt want. The Children's Sewing Society has its mission. Reform and benevolence, in whatever guise it works, benefits humanity and uplifts the race; for it does not only enhance the happiness of the recipient, but the donor as well. Money spent in benevolent purposes may always be put to the profit side of the account on our books; for in the great book of reckoning for eternity, every dollar spent for the glory of the race is placed to a man's credit."

CHAPTER V.

"I am persuaded that every time a man has a generous impulse—but much more when he performs a generous act—it adds something to generations yet to come."

While the band of earnest workers were devising plans to benefit the poor, a jeering crowd had assembled in Edna Proctor's home—a nice name for a **Pacific street den.**

" Well, Renwood, where's **your boy ?"**

" Gone."

" Police nab him ?"

" Yes; up for three months."

" Where's that gal of his ?

" Police got her, too.   **She is keeping company with Miff, as** usual.   **She is no good, always getting Miff into trouble."**

" **Your boy trained her, anyhow,"** said Mrs. Proctor.

" **Precious little training either one ever got,"** suggested John Martin.

" They're better than **yours, ever if you do send them to a** charity school."

" Better send them to **a charity school than the House of Correction,"** retorted Martin.

" **Miff can** take care of himself.   **He will make just as good a** man as your hypocritical **Sunday School children,"** Renwood replied.

" **Well, I propose to let my gals go** to Sunday **School, to Dr.** Halstead's **Reform School,** and wherever they please."

" Yes, and **you will have** them **puttin'** on airs, gettin' **converted, preachin' religion** and **takin'** away your liberties.   I'll

bet if your gals go to Sunday School you will quit coming here
within a month."

"It would'nt be much worse for me if I staid at home."

"You talk like a weak-kneed subject for emigrating right into
a church."

"It would be better for us all if we quit drinking and lived
better."

"Oh come, give us a regular sermon, won't you"? asked Ren_
wood.

"Take a drink first," suggested Mrs. Proctor.

The foaming beer and the destructive whiskey made them forget all about the sermon. Even Martin himself became noisy
and hilarious. A pale, sickly wife, poorly fed, and worse clad
children were forgotten. The revelry began. The hoodlums
passing were attracted by the hilarity. They stopped, entered
and were contaminated by vile companionship. They passed
out and on one square, perhaps two—another den, another
drink. Vile whisky had done its work. Alcohol in, every lingering fragment of good out. Before midnight they were in a
state of debauchery, that even paternal love would fall and con-
geal at the sight. A little girl came down the stairway at Proctor's saloon, and as she came into full view Renwood exclaimed:

"My God! how like her! Whose child is that?"

"Nobody's, I guess," was Mrs. Proctor's retort.

"Come here, little girl."

The child timidly approached him.

"What is your name?"

"Bona."

"Where do you live?"

"She lives with me, if you want to know," said Mrs. Proctor.

"I don't know why you need be so snappy about the girl."

"I don't know why you need be inquiring into other people's business," was the retort.

"Well, the child looks wonderfully like my poor dead Janey."

"Renwood, what became of that little daughter that my wife kept for you?"

"The charity people got her, and I never heard of her since."

"Do you remember she was called Bona. An odd name—perhaps the same one."

"Woman, where did you get this child?" demanded Renwood.

"She came here."

"Where from?"

- "Ask the girl."

"Bona, where do you live"

"Away off, at a place ever so much nicer than this. Won't you take me back to my mamma, please?"

"What is your mamma's name?"

"Other people call her Mrs. Benson."

"The very same," exclaimed Martin.

"I am your father, Bona." But years had separated the tie that binds, and the knowledge carried with it no paternal emotions.

Bona drew from him, and said: "No, you're not, for mamma told me I had'nt any father,"

"Now, see here, Renwood, I don't care whether she is your child or not. I have adopted her, and she stays right here with me. Bona, go upstairs and stay there. You should have been asleep long ago."

"Well, I guess not; Bona will go with me to-night."

"No, she won't."

Mrs. Proctor went over to where they were and led Bona away. Renwood was too cowardly to interfere, but he detained her long enough to imprint a kiss upon her pure lips. As she was led away, he arose and stole quietly from the room, like a man with a guilty conscience. The gentle touch of the child, Heaven's direct influence on wayward men, aroused the last fading, flickering spark of manhood within him. He started for his home—a room eight by ten—in a lodging house. He dreamed the dream of youth. Bad habits, whiskey and debauchery rob a man of the gifts of life; but the recollection of former days are the heritage of man, no matter what condition he may be in. It is the right of man in the hour of his greatest sorrow, even at the point where he ceases to be a man and becomes a brute, for the past with all its glorious achievements and happiest moments to rise up before him. Jared Renwood had felt the inspiration of youth; had tasted the joys of conscious power. The realization of brilliant hopes stood but a little distance from him. In a moment of temptation he threw off the restraints which are placed upon every man. The transformation from manhood to mere brute existence was rapid indeed. The touch of lips to lips, the angel touch of Bona, as her hand, so small, so soft and caressing, rested a moment on his bleared and sin-marked face, aroused within him the thoughts and emotions which visit the degenerate only at rare intervals. Renwood promised the impulse to lead a nobler life. He remained three days, and then he was back at Proctor's again, drinking and carousing worse than ever. A youth will, a young man may—an old man hardly ever does reform.

A training school for children, a reform school for youths, a house of correction for young men, a penitentiary for men; and these institutions, properly conducted, may regulate society; but the solution to the great social problem is found in Bona's reply to Mrs. Proctor.

" Here, drink this beer."

" Mamma taught me never to do that."

" Drink, I say."

3

"No, I wont, for mamma said I shouldn't taste anything like that."

"Well, well, such training; they will soon be trying to make us all saints."

The teaching of love had more power than the influence of fear, and Bona, with the Christian culture of ten years, stood out firmly against the woman's demands. Bona had been in care of Mrs. Proctor several months. Dr. Halstead and Mrs. Benson had tried in vain to find her. They inquired of Mrs. Proctor and Renwood, but they consciously lied to them. Yet both Dr. Halstead and Mrs. Benson were convinced the child was in their possession, but they had no way to get possession of her. Oswald Grayson now enters the story again. In the meantime he had not been idle. Many useful men and women will remember how they were helped, comforted and aided by his generous acts. When asked why he spent his time among the lower classes and worked differently from other people—for the world knew of his charity—he responded: "I am persuaded that every time a man has a generous impulse—but much more when he performs a generous act—it adds something to generations yet to come. Yes, I am convinced that the highest degree of personal happiness is found in bestowing happiness upon others."

One day, as Grayson was passing down Pacific street, he saw Bona in the saloon, and entering, learned, by stealth, her position. He received a permit for the girl, and an official order to place her in the Home of the Friendless. The institution was presided over by a fat, fussy and grumbling woman, whose face wore a perpetual scowl. Perhaps the best insight into the whole institution can be gained from Bona's diary. Mrs. Benson taught her to write something each day—a record of the day's work. How well she performed her part can be learned from the following:

CHAPTER VI.

"Error does not stop where it begins. The misdeeds of youth are the crimes of maturer years."

"TUESDAY, June 11th. —There are lots of girls and boys here. They are watched by ugly women, who beat and scold them. At meals they eat with fingers, and always eat so fast they can't talk. I know it is wrong to do that way, because mamma told me it was. Last night a nice little girl died— the one that the ugly woman whipped yesterday. I think the people are cruel. I wish they would speak kindly, instead of harsh and cruel. Mrs. Lamor orders us around just like our old coal man did his horse. When Mr. Grayson comes, I am going to coax him to take me away. I know that he will find mamma. I hear a lot of boys and girls being whipped in the hall. I wish they would not cry so. I am going to run away from this horrid place. That's all for to-day. BONA."

The leaves of her diary were stained with tears. Bona's running comment each day was something like the preceding—the wail of woe, the consciousness of poverty, and the complete lack of sympathy. Better for the helpless poor to die upon the cold and cheerless street; to lift their hands in mute appeal to Heaven, and receive naught else in return but the rain or the morning dew, than to die unloved and a burden to the miscalled charitable institutions of this city. The cry of the children re-echoes from Heaven in the ears of God's people. They heed it not, unless perchance the echo resounds in the heart of some sympathetic woman, who labors patiently and earnestly for the good of neglected youths. The rich—those who have by successful speculation reached the sphere of luxury—will pay hundreds of dollars for a mere luxury, and a dollar or two is all that they give, and that grudgingly, to the deserving poor. The wheels of Juggernaut should crush out of existence every parsimonious heart. Human nature once touched with the fair caress of charity is warm and tender, but oh, the cold exterior which

bars the approach of a generous impulse. A man may commit
suicide and yet live. He crushes out of existence every fragment of happiness, when he strangles the promptings of a generous heart. While one stops to moralize, the world moves on.
The rich change places with the poor; the child becomes a man,
and the man returns to the dust. The street waif has become
calloused by repeated crimes, and the good have grown nobler
by their self-sacrifice.

*   *   *   *   *   *   *   *

Five years have passed—five long years—since Miff and Viola
were sentenced to the House of Correction. They still follow
their old way of living. Error does not stop where it begins.
The misdeeds of youth are the crime of maturer years.

One morning when the fog made the city almost dark, the re-
gion of the Barbary Coast was cheerless and drear. The inhabi-
tants seldom retired before the town clock had struck two, hence
it was late in the day before they arose. A solitary figure half-
walked, half-sneaked along Pacific street. Her old dress, faded,
tattered and torn, hung upon her ill-shaped form. Her beauty
was marred by strong lines of dissipation, her eyes lined with
dark rings, and the sparkle removed by the presence of blood.
Her walk was a swagger, her looks revealed the sadness of her
heart, and her whole existence seemed to be within the circle of
shameful dissipation. On up the street until the jail is reached;
then boldly going up to the guard, she asked:

"Is Miff here?"

She knew no other name for him, and no other name is needed,
because the good and the bad alike know a notorious character
by his first name.

"What do you want with him?" was the guard's reply.

An old woman passing by tapped Viola on the chin. "Well,
my beauty, come after your lover, did yer? Better look up an-

other. They are no good once in there." And she pointed her long, bony finger towards the dingy cells.

Viola drew back from the woman's presence. Soon a released prisoner came out, but it was not Miff.

"Hello," he said. And leered at her, while she drew further back.

At last, unable to bear the scrutiny of the crowd, she went in the corner, and stood obscured by the open door. As each one passed, she looked for Miff. While watching, Oswald Grayson passed in. She stepped from the corner, and touched him on the sleeve. He turned.

"Why, is this you, Viola?"

"Yes. Miff is in there. Won't you get him out for me?"

"I once said that if you were ever in trouble, I would help you. It has been nearly two years since I saw you. You and Miff are still together? Well, well, ever since you were cherubs in the cellar at the old house, I have watched you, but my efforts to reform you have all been in vain. I am afraid Heaven will have to make special arrangements for such as you."

"Don't talk that way. I want Miff. We are not bad. Miff is real good. He never hurts any one, but we must' get a living somehow."

"There comes Miff." And in a minute Viola was by his side and nodding to Grayson. They passed on through the corridors and out. Miff had just completed a six months' sentence in jail.

"Come, let us go to our den," said Miff, gruffly; "I am anxious to see how it looks after six months' absence. Do you know, Viola, I missed you every day?"

In turn for such a wonderful exhibition of tenderness on the part of Miff, Viola gently pressed his hand and raised her eyes to his. Long since they had ceased to kiss each other. Such a token of affection belongs strictly to the pure. Now and then they did not forget the sympathy aroused by the touch of trembling lips, but it was not an every day occurrence, as it is where love and refinement exist.

As they went up the stairway, Miff's heart seemed to awaken to new life. As they stood side by side in the doorway, Miff stooped and celebrated his return by a kiss that almost shamed the untidy and unladylike appearance of Viola. In return Viola threw her arms about his neck and said: "I am awful glad to have yer back again. We won't let the police ketch you another time."

"Were you lonesome when I was away?"

"I was so miserable that I had a notion to throw myself in the bay."

"Well, I am glad we are together again. Say, have you got anything good to eat or drink?"

"Here's your favorite whisky."

"Let us go and have some lunch somewhere. Well, you still have those violets. Why do you keep them?"

"I don't know. For years and years I loved them; and do you know that whenever I am real hungry I dream about such a beautiful place, all covered with flowers, just like the place that we heard about the day we went to the Children's Hall?"

"That was a long time ago."

"Yes; but we were happier then than now."

"We will be happy again Just wait; I will make a big strike one of these days."

"Even if you do, it will be all the same. We live, eat and drink. I don't know what we live for, if we must always be this way. I wish I had drowned myself, I am so tired of life."

"You must not talk that way—I am back again."

"Yes, I know; but what of that? Must we not go on as ever before? There is nothing to do but prowl round the streets, and take whatever we can put our fingers on. It's drink, and sleep, and steal; that's all of livin'. When I saw poor, crippled Jennie dead, and her white face turned toward the sky, I thought she must be awful happy, to look so peaceful. Nobody cares for us, and I am tired of being hammered about. If it wasn't for you, I would die."

"Take some of this, and then we will go on a visit to the old places again."

He handed her the jug of whisky. She drank deeply. A false and artificial life was infused into her veins. She was stirred to action. Thoughts of death were far removed. Her contemplation began and ended within the limits of the present. The past and the future were as dimly outlined as the horizon on a misty morning. She was herself again, and, being so, she was certainly not an attractive character.

Viola hastily pushed the chair into a corner, picked up a few knicknacks, closed the outer door, and, taking Miff's arm, pulled him towards the stairway. As they entered upon the street, walking side by side, she was as proud as a queen, and no sweetheart was ever as proud of her lover as Viola was of Miff, as he made his first appearance since he had been in jail. It was rumored, and no doubt the rumor was true, that Miff served the sentence that Viola should in justice have received. The night was dark, and it was an unfrequented part of the city. An old dress was stolen. It was discovered in Viola's room. Miff acknowledged the theft and suffered the penalty. Whether Miff or Viola stole the dress is not known.

"There's that pretty girl that brought me nice flowers, and was so kind to me," said Miff. He made an awkward attempt to bow, and the lady smiled graciously.

"My! but ain't she a proud thing," exclaimed Viola.

"Why, no; she ain't proud, or she wouldn't have come to the jail with flowers, and treated me so nicely."

"People pay her for doing that."

"No, they don't."

"Well, that old preacher on the corner used to say that it paid to be good."

Miff gave rather an irreverent laugh, as he said: "I have often heard about rewards for the good, but did not know that they got any coin."

They were on the lookout for something to eat. They had no money. Viola had held fast to her empty pouch. They passed Edna Proctor's place, when they heard a cry of sudden pain within. They entered. Renwood was lying upon his face; the blood was oozing from a wound in the back. Miff, hastily turning him over, saw the pale, deathly face of his father.

"I am dying; she did it," he gasped, and died.

A crowd gathered in the saloon. A doctor arrived. The cut was a terrible one; the rib was severed as though a surgeon had performed the operation. The knife lay upon the floor, reeking with blood.

Edna Proctor gave her testimony to the people as follows: "I was in the back room, and I heard Renwood quarreling with some Chinamen about some money. Renwood could talk the Chinese language some, and of course I could not tell what they were quarreling about; but as I came to the door one of the Chinamen drew his knife and stabbed him in the back. Then they all ran off."

The woman's story was listened to attentively. The policeman began a search for some evidence of Chinese presence. They picked up the knife; it had a long blade, sharp on both sides and tapered to a round point—a deadly weapon in the hands of the assassin. It was undoubtedly a Chinese knife.

Miff looked upon the face of his murdered father unmoved; Viola stood trembling by his side.

" Don't tell, will you ?"

" Yes; your mother killed the old man."

" If you tell, they will put her in jail—perhaps hang her like they did Mrs. Rankin when she killed her man. If you tell, I'll throw myself into the bay."

" What business had she to stab him, anyway."

" They quarreled; you know you hit me once when you were mad."

" I'm going to tell, anyway."

" If you do, I'll murder you."

A fierce light came into her eye. She clutched his arm. Her fingers tightened with a vise-like grip, and the nails were imbedded in the calloused skin. With her right hand she drew a knife; it flashed as she drew it back.

Miff touched her arm and said: " Well, if you care for the old woman so much as that, I will keep mum."

They came from the side room. The Coroner had arrived; the verdict was given: " Came to his death by the stab of a knife in the hands of an unknown Chinaman."

All that was mortal of Jared Renwood was borne from the saloon. A life of degradation met its legitimate end; the hand of the ruffian had struck the blow. For twenty years Jared Renwood had lived on the Barbary Coast. His being was dead long ago to the finer sensibilities that govern humanity. His rough habits and dissipated manner of living killed a gentle creature, his wife, ruined his son Miff, and eternally damned himself. No monument points heavenward over his grave; his deeds are celebrated by the wickedness of his son Miff. A proper epitaph over such a grave would be: " He lived a disgrace to humanity, and his end was like unto his life. God pity such."

A policeman watched closely the saloon of Edna Proctor. Two Chinamen passed on the other side of the street; they were notorious highbinders. "That's them, quick!" exclaimed Mrs. Proctor.

The policeman followed the Chinamen to the corner, and just as they turned down Sansome street he blew his whistle, and, exhibiting his club, arrested them.

"Me no stealee, me no killee, me no anything."

CHAPTER VII.

" If the original state of woman is represented by the lowest element of society, it would be better for humanity had Adam never lost a rib."

The prompt, inconsiderate denial of a charge is a half confession. The thief cries out aloud, "I took it not." The murderer declares, "I did not kill him." The child before condemned will plead "not guilty." The nature of man is but the exemplification of the weaknesses of childhood. The terrible charge of murder was placed against the two Chinamen. They denied it so strenuously that the authorities were convinced of their guilt. On the preliminary examination a true bill was found, and they were consigned to the dingiest and most criminal cell in the prison. A Chinaman, whether innocent or guilty, deserves no better fate. Do you suppose they feel? Would an insinuation bare and cruel touch the sensibilities beneath their yellow skin? Are they not dead to pain? Do they laugh, smile or cry? Would a slap, a blow or a beating injure their hardened natures? If you meet a Chinaman, spit at him, or trip him up and see him fall on his face. If you want exercise, throw sticks and stones at him; he will be amused thereby. The Chinese are a queer race. If in a foreign country an unfriendly hand is laid upon an American shoulder, the whole American nation declares that its citizens must be protected. A low woman who stands behind the bar of a groggery, who neither recognizes the responsibilities of her being nor of an oath—to her a lie is smart, a truth stupid, a crime shrewd, a noble deed but the exhibition of weakness—the testimony of such a woman placed the two Chinamen in jail, where for weeks they existed, like entrapped animals.

Edna Proctor felt that she was free. Little did she dream that her daughter and Miff possessed the secret of her terrible crime. But she was not permitted to rest in her fancied security long, for one morning Miff entered the room, and, approaching the counter, spoke in a commanding voice:

"Give me some money, old woman!"

"Indeed, you had better get out," replied Mrs. Proctor.

"I want five dollars."

"I won't give you five cents."

"If you don't give me the money, I will tell who killed my father." And the words fairly hissed through his lips.

"What!" And over the dissipated face came the paleness of great and heart-rending fear.

"I know all. If you give me the money, I'll be silent."

Mrs. Proctor opened the drawer, and placed upon the box the money. Miff picked up the large silver dollars, counting: "One, two, three, four, five—right, old woman. When I want money again, you must be quicker, or I'll let out on you."

"You had better not come here again for money, because you'll not get any more."

"Don't be too sure. This will go for the support of your daughter. I will want some for myself after awhile."

Just as Miff stepped out, Oswald Grayson appeared at the door.

"Hello, young man. How are you getting on?" And he took Miff's hand in his and gave it a welcome shake.

They re-entered the saloon. Mr. Grayson bid Mrs. Proctor a pleasant good morning, and asked leave to place some reading matter on her tables. She gave him the permission, but he had no sooner gone away than she gathered up the papers and put them into the stove. Good literature is the strongest influence the disseminators of vice have to contend against.

" Miff, do you know that we would all be better men if there were no such women as that?"

" I am sure she hasn't done me any good."

"Twenty years ago your father was a good, hard-working man, loved by the noblest woman on earth, and I loved that woman there. Your mother was one of the best women that ever lived, and was so kind to your father. But an evil day came, and he was ruined by bad men and women. Your mother died partly of a broken heart, and your father took up with Mrs. Proctor, and in her den was killed. Miff, you are going the same way. Unless you face about, you will end your days either in prison, on the gallows or in a saloon brawl. Learn a lesson from the sad death of your father. There is a whole volume of instruction in it for you, you know—" But Miff could not stand any more. The sentence was finished mentally. He left Grayson very suddenly, and in a few moments was in a saloon, drowning the thoughts to which Grayson's words gave rise by the vilest of vile whisky. Grayson walked on down Pacific street on his mission of good, distributing here and there his papers. The flippant man will laugh at the benefactor, and in his self-wisdom will knowingly talk of wasted energies in the furtherance of good, yet Sunday, when Miff and Viola were in their room together, they planned a trip to the wharf where Miff had noticed a box, which they could open with a hatchet and take its contents. The plan was matured, when Miff drew one of Grayson's tracts, and read the words, "Thou shalt not steal." That night they wandered around to the Children's Home, and entered. They listened to the songs; they heard a prayer, and the words of the speaker fell with power upon their untrained minds. It was a novelty to them. They left strongly impressed, and returned, instead of to a saloon, to spend the night in ribaldry and dissipation, to their rooms. It seemed the good people of the city had cast their nets, and they were caught at every turn. The fishers of men, if the prosecutors labored as faithfully as the Chinese fishermen on this coast, would fill their nets from the stagnant sloughs of society.

"I say, Viola, let us get married?" said Miff, abruptly, as they reached their room.

"How?"

"Why, let us go, like Mr. and Mrs. Jarvis, to the Justice, and get married by law. Then we could live legally together."

"Does getting married make us quarrel like such people? You be my husband, and I be your wife. Mam had a husband once, and he beat her awfully. No; I don't want any husband. You are good enough for me."

"Yes; but you know it is a sin, and they could put us in jail for being this way."

"Why, we lived this way ever since I can remember, and nobody ever said anything."

"Yes; but we are getting older now, and indeed it is wicked. That beautiful girl who came to me in jail said we ought to marry."

"I don't like her. I don't see why you are always calling her pretty—she ain't."

"She was awful good to me. When she touched my hand I felt queer. She said she would be a sister to me, if I would work and quit stealing. Every time I meet her—why, do you know?—she looks like my mother. I know now—I used to think I knew some one who looked like her. I remember now, mother—my mother. It was so long, long ago—long before I remember you—that she died. That beautiful girl is just like her."

There was a bond of sympathy between Bona and Miff that

those unacquainted with their history could not understand. Viola was jealous, bitterly jealous; for years and years Miff had praised only her. Now, he talked of the beauty of Bona; heretofore he was in sympathy only with Viola. All the world to him was cold, formal, disheartening; everybody was against him, and he was against everybody. Is it any wonder that between Miff and Viola there should be an intense love?

"Come, Miff, let us go to the theater to-night?" said Viola, after a successful day of plundering.

"We are not fit to go to a nice theater."

"Yes; we are, if we buy our seats."

"I am afraid they will put us out, unless we go to the gallery; and if we go up there, the boys will laugh at us, and you don't want to be laughed at."

"I don't care for once, and I do want to see a real big theater and see the things that are in the pictures on the fence."

"Well, we will go to-night, then; but if any of the fellows make fun of us, I'll fight."

They stood at the entrance, and saw the fashionably dressed people enter. The young men and sweethearts, and old men and maidens, sons, mothers, wives and fathers, daughters and children, all entered, happy in their companionship, happy in anticipation of the famous actors' interpretation of one of Shakspeare's greatest dramas.

"Wouldn't I like to be dressed as them folks!"

"Come," said Miff, "let us go in."

They went up the narrow stairway to the gallery, and crowded in among the hoodlums gathered there. Viola gazed in admiration upon the adornments of the theater. She had visited variety shows, music halls and low places of amusement, but she had never been in a grand theater before. Everything was new to her. The curtain was rung up; the play began.

Soon a beautiful girl came on the stage; words of love were spoken; a betrothal ring was placed upon her finger; a kiss, a promise, a pledge; and then the acts in the drama came on. At last the beautiful girl, dressed like a boy, came upon the stage searching for her lover. At almost every turn applause greeted her; all eyes watched the grace and ease of her every movement. They listened breathlessly to the sweet cadences of her voice. The turn of her beautiful eyes, the twitch of her fingers, the expression of her face were observed—yes, the gaze of the audience was fixed upon the beautiful actress. No one cared for the King Cymbeline.

"But don't I wish I was her," whispered Viola.

"Keep quiet," replied Miff.

"Look at her now; there she comes down the mountain. Can't she hollow nicely, though?'

"Keep quiet," said Miff.

"I am going to be an actress. Oh, but wouldn't I like to have people look at me that way!"

"Keep quiet," said Miff.

"Isn't that grand, though?"

"There is Bona."

"Where?"

"Away down there, aside a young man, near that corner."

"It's queer how you see her every place. You'll soon be leaving me and running after her."

The curtain was rung down. Viola had seen and heard, and she had an ardent desire to be an actress—a great actress. The play aroused her to new life.

"Miff, I am going to quit stealing. I am going to go on the stage," said Viola, as they reached their room.

"You're too old, and you don't know anything. You can't be an actress. Why, I don't know enough myself to do like they did on the stage to-night. They're great people. I guess we had better keep on **stealing**."

They did **keep on** plotting **and** planning. **Even the theater** taught the **two** something. They were inspired by **the** play; they were invited to live a higher and nobler life. **After** all, Shakspeare did not write in vain, and our magnificent theaters were not built to retard the progress of the race. The ignorant are even entertained by **that** which delights **the** highly educated. There **is** not much **difference** between the learned and the un-learned. That **which divides the classes is** not an impassable **barrier; it is** simply **a mere** circumstance that rises up between **the two, and** can be **removed at** will. True, the will **is** some-times wanting, but it can be attained.

" **Stay here, Viola, until I go out and** get some more **money. Do you** know I have **a real** mine up the street? Whenever **I say ' Gold '** silver appears. I found the mine about two weeks ago."

" Mayn't I go long and see **it?** "

" No; you would spoil it all. I must be alone."

Miff started, and in **a few** moments **was** in the presence of Mrs. Proctor.

" I want some more money, old woman."

" You get out of this."

" Well, **I** guess I'll go and see how much the police will give **me** if I tell the whole story. Must have five dollars."

" **If I** give you that, will you promise not to bother me any **more ?"**

" Yes."

" **Here,** take **it and** go, and if you come back, I'll use you worse than I did your drunken father. Mind, now, what I say; you keep yourself scarce—do you hear?" And she drew from a hidden pocket a dangerous looking knife.

4

CHAPTER VIII.

"A sympathetic cord runs from a generous heart to the pocket, and no man has a patent on nobility until he can truthfully say, 'I give cheerfully.'"

Who can explain the affinity of souls? A strange, peculiar feeling came over Miff every time he met Bona. He wept over the sensation; the hard nature was touched; upon his eyelids glistened not one tear, as he beheld the corpse of his murdered father, yet tears rolled down his cheeks, and sweat stood upon his forehead like the oozing sap from a bruised reed, as he realized the unbridgeable gulf between Bona and himself. Strange, yet nevertheless true, he worshiped her purity, and turned away in disgust from Viola, who, like fruit ripened in the shade, became bitter. Oh, ye generations of men! oh, of vipers! why will you make impure, and then turn in disgust and worship purity?

Miff's whole nature thrilled with passionate love for Bona, and he wept at the folly of his passion. He could not steal, he hated whisky, shunned the company of his former associates, neglected Viola, and despised his unwashed hands and unkempt hair; he tore his ragged pants, and gazed with heart-bursting envy upon the well-dressed men.

"If I could be better, I would," he declared to himself again and again. Then he thought it was no use, and caressed, with more tenderness than ever before, the almost heart-broken Viola.

"Oh, Miff, if you follow that girl, the bay is waiting for me. I'll never, never leave you go," passionately responded Viola.

"I like you, Viola, better than I do her; but it seems as though I must touch her hand, or kiss her forehead," said Miff, as he gently impressed a kiss on Viola's brow.

But, alas, the demon of despondency crept over Miff, the forerunner of crime and suicide. He refused to steal or to beg; they both went hungry, sometimes for days, for weeks. Miff grew pale, emaciated. One night he did not return home. Viola watched; he had promised to bring her some food; she was afraid to go out and steal. She watched the tallow dip burn until the flickering wick refused to give forth light. She waited, oh, so wearily, but he did not come. At last her head fell heavily towards her breast; she slept. She dreamed Miff was being led away to jail; he had robbed a man, struck him a blow, and left him lying bleeding on the street. She rushed after the men, begged them not to take him to prison, pleaded with them, and, growing desperate, fought, and in her dream she seemed to succeed. A gleam of triumph overspread her face; she smiled in her sleep—a wicked smile of triumph—as she dragged Miff away from the police. Every step she seemed to fall; while running at full speed, she did not seem to get away. Great fear came over her; she felt the heavy club of the policeman upon her head; she saw the blood running upon the ground. "I'm dying, I am dying," she muttered audibly; then awoke to fully realize her loneliness.

She put on her old bonnet, and started out upon the deserted streets to find Miff. She looked in alleys, peeped in saloons; now and then stole inside and picked up a handful of crackers or something from a free lunch counter. On, on she wandered in darkness. The night was calm and still; the gas jets burned luminously; now and then some vagabond would be returning to his home; again, some business man who had studied until the morning hours over his books. No one bothered Viola; the policemen looked at her askance, but she cast at them a defiant glance, and passed on inquiring to herself, "Miff, O Miff, where are you?" She left the streets and wandered down by the water front. She looked in the low saloons, in some underground

traps; she looked in every place bad, and went on in the darkness, sometimes murmuring aloud, "Miff, Miff," then sadly
moaning, "I wish he would come."

But she did not wait. From place to place she wandered,
until the morning sun conquered the last ray of darkness, and
light overspread the city. Then she wearily turned her steps
homeward. As she stood at the foot of the stairway and glanced
up, she beheld Miff lying half-way to the top, the stairs bloody,
and Miff silent, unconscious, perhaps dead. Quickly she sprang
to his side, as though the sight of the blood had nerved her like
an electric shock. She took his head in her lap and bathed the
blood-stained face in tears. She knew no God to whom she could
raise her eyes and implore aid. A fierce light came into her eyes.
Her broad forehead seemed split in two by the blue vein across
it, that swelled in anger until the blood became purple. She
was pale as death; her eyes became tearless and dull as a stone.
With the sudden strength that occasion brings, she lifted him up
tenderly in her arms, and carried him to the room. She placed
him on the old mattress, and, taking off her woolen skirt, folded
it and made her unconscious lover a pillow. She bathed the
wounded spot, and tried to stop the flow of blood, but it flowed
on. She knew that it had to be stopped, and, seizing her un-
combed hair, she tore it in frenzy from her head, the pain almost
making the eyeballs protrude from their sockets. She matted
the hair in blood, and placed it over the wound, and then, stoop-
ing low, kissed the clotted hunk of hair. It had stopped the flow
of blood. "Miff is saved," she thought, for did she not feel the
beating of his heart against her bosom? For a moment she
left. She hurried down to a saloon, and, gliding in, seized a
bottle of brandy before the astonished barkeeper had time to
think about the matter. In a moment she was pouring the
brandy down Miff's throat. The barkeeper of course followed

the thief, but his hard heart was touched as he looked upon the scene. A crowd gathered. The poverty of the place was noticed. Many who had not the money to buy a meal dropped their bit in the barkeeper's hand, as he said, "Let's help them out; poor girl, looks as though she was starving."

Bona came and brought a flower; she placed it upon Miff's breast. Viola, in jealous rage, threw it out of the window. She kissed Miff's pallid lips as a mother kisses the dead corpse of her child, and, placing her arm over Miff, turned to Bona, and, with all the vehemence of her misguided nature, said: "Go 'way; he is mine, all mine; you can't have him—leave me alone."

Bona drew back in surprise; the whole truth burst upon her at once. She knew the secret of Miff's peculiar power over her; Miff loved her, and this girl was jealous.

"I will not take him from you; I came to restore him to you. I brought this and this," she said, as she unpacked some tempting delicacies. "You stay with him, and I will go and send a doctor, and perhaps get some money for you, so that he will not need to be removed to the hospital," and going to Viola, she kindly extended her hand, but Viola turned her back.

Bona had consecrated her life to useful work. Strange has been the experience, but upon the matured woman can be seen the early training of Mrs. Benton. Despair not, faithful mother, for the well-being of your child, if you have trained it aright in its infancy.

Bona went direct to Dr. Halstead and told him about the two unfortunates. The good and generous doctor immediately gave her twenty-five dollars for the use of Miff and Viola. As Bona received the money, she turned to the Doctor, and, with one of her sweetest smiles, said: "Remember, Doctor, that I believe that there is a sympathetic cord between a generous heart and the pocket, and no man has a patent on nobility unless he can say, 'I give cheerfully.' I think, Doctor, that you have the most improved patent upon nobility, but I trust, for the sake of humanity, that others will infringe upon it."

The Doctor replied, modestly: "You have no reason to suspect a man of being generous, if he has means so to be."

Bona left with the money in her hand, and hurried back to the cheerless home, anticipating the pleasure of giving Viola the money. When she entered the room, Viola greeted her warmly, and, going to her, said: "I was bad this morning. I know you are good, and I should not hate you because Miff likes you so well."

Viola had gone down on the street and picked up the crushed flower, and placed it again on Miff's breast.

"Hush!" said Viola, "he moves."

Miff struggled a little, and then opened his eyes and looked around the room. Bona noticed the clotted hair, and, looking at Viola, saw the bare spot upon her head, the blood oozing out from where the hair had been pulled.

"Truly, she must love him. I will never more despise the bad, because in moments of great trials they prove themselves superior beings."

CHAPTER IX.

"Always the whisky! forever the one terrible curse, dragging men down. Always the awful, soul-destroying curse—drink, from which the nation will make no mighty effort to free itself, and save itself. And like a cloud before the destructive storm, it gathers force and God's lightnings."

Viola was at last left alone with Miff. Soon a group of men from the saloon came kindly in to see if they could assist. Human nature is kind, full of pity, full of sympathy, but wonderfully cold, if you neither rise above nor sink below its level. Miff grew worse; his eyes opened and rolled, his legs quivered.

"Can't some of you pray?" asked Viola.

How many in the motley group were reminded of the prayer at the mother's knee? How many were carried back to the distant home, perchance to some old farm-house, yet where peace and content loved to dwell? At last one said that he could pray. He had not forgotten—what our fashionable people have —to kneel. The rough men took off their hats, and are we mistaken that a tear glistened in many an eye? Why, no; it rolled down the cheek, washing a furrow as it flowed. Sober, silent and reverent in the presence of death, these men who reviled the church felt the awful presence of God as they bowed their heads.

The man began to pray: "O Lord"—His courage forsook him, and he could make no other appeal. He arose and shrunk out of the room, guilty sinner that he was. Then another, bolder and seemingly more devout than the rest, tried it. He kneeled at Miff's side and began:

"I lay me down to sleep"—He thought he heard an irreverent companion laughing; he left and started to the saloon—the way of all sinners. The humble petition, perhaps, reached as near Heaven as the rhetorical prayer from a book. The men were dismayed. The doctor arrived; their fears were groundless—Miff was seriously, though not mortally, wounded. "This has saved his life," said the doctor, as he raised the clotted hair from the wound. "Your act has proven your affection as great as that of the Cynthian maiden, who buried her lover and her beautiful curls together."

Viola smiled gratefully. The trouble had made her wonderfully tender and kind. The fierce, wild light of her eye was subdued, and she hailed with gladness the news of Miff's probable recovery. Oswald Grayson heard of Miff's wound, and hurried to his side. Miff was able to converse. He told his story in a sad, pitiful way; his words were freighted with despair, his voice was tuned to the wail of despondency, as he said: "For two long weeks I have tried to do without drink. Oh, the terrible agony I endured. I felt like a fish on the mountain top; my throat burned. I felt the strength of my nerves oozing through my skin. My eyes seemed to grow dim. I felt as though I should die. Driven to despair, I entered a saloon, and drank and drank until fire burned in my veins. I had a fight and was stabbed, and that is why I am here almost dead."

"But you will get well again, Miff," said Viola.

"I hope not," was his despondent answer.

"Always the whisky," said Grayson, "forever the one terrible curse, dragging men down. Always the awful, soul-destroying curse—drink, from which the nation will make no mighty effort to free itself and save itself. And, like a cloud before a destructive storm, it gathers force and God's lightnings."

If you have ever laughed scornfully at a temperance fanatic, remember the cause and not its advocate. Reforms in society are made by the extremes of evils. If you are a matter-of-fact man, take up a morning newspaper; we will wait while you read: "A man kicked his wife brutally, because she reproved him for drinking up his week's wages and leaving her to starve;" but that is the old story—drink. "A poor, crazy fellow hanged himself in a police cell"—all drink. "A drunken woman dropped her baby out of the window." "A man was found crushed upon the railroad track; supposed to be drunk." But these are the ordinary day's doings. They possess nothing new to the toper, nor to others; the work of the drink-devil is too familiar to all. He strikes down his victims in daylight as well as under cover of darkness. The innocent youth is not too small to receive his notice, nor is the statesman too great. He invades not only the home; the political arena is his dwelling place as well. When will the nation rise in its might and crush out the monster curse? Let us chain the drink-devil in the bottomless pit forever and forever. Let us tear down the Temple of Bacchus and build churches and schools. The shadow of death—the shadow of evil—lurks on every corner. A saloon, like the devil, is always at a man's elbow. Miff's tragedy had no especial horror—a man struck down in a drunken brawl in a saloon—yet the horrors born of drink are a shame to this, a Christian nation.

Oswald Grayson was more than ever in earnest in his work. He saw before him a man whom he had tried to save; he saw that he was working almost in vain for the myriads of weaklings drifting with the current to their soul's discomfiture. To the next man he met he presented his tract as though it were a pistol, and demanded the man's reformation or his life.

In another part of the city a different scene was enacted. The appointed hour had arrived for the convicted murderers of Jared Renwood. The two Chinamen stood at the entrance of another world; the latch-string, the hangman's rope, hung above their heads. In a few minutes they would be hanged. The yellow

countenances paled; they feared death, and trembled violently
at its approach. They declared, "Me no killee," not with a
defiant air, but piteously, tremblingly, mournfully. True, the
evidence was not strong against them, but it requires very little
to convict Chinamen. Detestation of a prisoner is three-fourths
conviction. The Chinaman cannot cry out like Paul, "I am
a Roman." His nationality is his grievous crime. No respite
was granted them, no pardon, no delay, no insanity plea; they
must die, and die quickly. The Sheriff, of course, had sympathy for them; the butcher hates to hear the dying pig squeal,
the hangman likewise pities his victims.

Grayson mentioned to Miff that his father's murderers would
be hanged that day. Miff was visibly affected; Viola turned
pale.

"We must save them," Miff said.

"How?" asked Viola.

"We must tell who killed my father."

"Then mam will be hanged. No, no! I can't see her treated
that way."

"But would you let two Chinamen die, when they are innocent? They won't hang your mother."

"They are only Chinamen, anyhow."

"Well, I don't care; I am going up to report, and you go
tell your wicked mother to clear out, or she will be arrested."

Miff, still weak, started towards the jail. He met a policeman, and told him the story; but the knowing guardian did not
believe the story, and Miff hurried on. The wound bled afresh,
the pain increased, but still he hastened on. At last Viola over-
took him, and they proceeded to the jail. They hurriedly told
their story. The jailer led them out in the yard. The Chinamen had just been cut down. Miff and Viola gazed on their
purple faces, and knew the Chinamen were dead; they had paid

the penalty of prejudice—the penalty of accepting the invitation of a great Christian nation to enjoy the freedom and the advantage of a republican government. Miff told his story, but it was too late. Sad words—too late—fraught with peril and years of regret. The law was appeased, and for the interest of the justice of law the correctness of its verdicts, its dignity and majesty, but little effort was made to bring Mrs. Proctor to justice; and the true state of the case in this age of newspapers was never made public.

Miff and Viola were affected by the scene, and quietly they returned to their dingy room. They hardly spoke; events began to make them thoughtful. As they walked along the crowded streets, they were as much alone as if on the mountain top. Their lives had arrayed them against humanity; they were completely alone. A thief may love company, but not confidants. The young man who has no friends, and lives an honest, upright life, is deserving of greater honor than the one hedged in to noble principles by a circle of friends.

When Miff and Viola reached Proctor's saloon, they found the place deserted. Mrs. Proctor had fled; an old man stood behind the counter ready to wait upon the miserable customers. He was dirty and palsy-stricken, with gray hair matted about his head and trailing in wiry streaks about his eyes. He was a shambling, half-drunken shadow of a man, the reflex of hundreds of men one sees at low saloon counters, or reeling through the back streets of San Francisco, helpless and degraded atoms of humanity. Why such men exist is a question time deals with leniently.

"The old woman is gone," said Miff. "Glad of it; better for her." And they left the saloon, looking rather fearlessly at the whisky-sodden man in charge.

CHAPTER X.

"There is an eternal warfare between education and nature—between society and the natural man. It begins when we first lisp "A, B, C," and the smoke of the battle clears away only when we cross into the kingdom beyond."

Mental struggles are the fiercest. The mind heralds the impulses of the heart. Between the mind and the heart there is no contest. The warfare exists between the mind and nature. Strong men laugh at the fancy. Yet we have seen man's nature turn against him, and with a cruel weapon pierce his heart, until, like the drooping flower, he withered into dust. Miff and Viola had joined the struggle. They had met the foe. Their minds, though weak, were awakened. The influence of Grayson, Bona and Dr. Halstead had moved them. For twenty long years their consciences had been as dormant as those of the soulless animals, and their deeds as wicked as the inclinations of conscienceless beings could make them. Somehow they now felt that the death of the two Chinamen was the result of their action. They trembled; they looked at each other, and crime was the intelligence in the look.

Miff, as he walked along, would sight over his shoulder like a practiced hunter, fearing at each corner an officer. They entered their cheerless room, sad and disconsolate. They turned in disgust from the hoodlum howling a ribald song from deadfalls—the fast, inane composition, which the verdict of an inane audience had rendered popular. The words were of woman's infidelity—base mockery of a base man. The praise of woman's fidelity is sung by angels in Heaven; her infidelity is applauded by every deadfall, every dive, every low saloon in this city. Some righteous men will point the fingers of scorn at Viola. The flower of the street when budding was beautiful, but it was crushed. How could it blossom on the street, and give out a delicious perfume. Yet, though crushed, stamped upon, smothered by weeds, rank, foul and overpowering the flower, preserved its characteristics, for Viola was blessed with the divine attribute, fidelity. She was as true to Miff as nature is to its laws. Their union was as strong as though bound by civil law. They were as much one as though the priest had blessed their union.

They were married as surely as the mingling of souls, as the union of spirit, as the communion of natures, weds two lives together. They were bound by a mightier cord than that of a justice of the peace, because to break the bonds of love you break hearts, but to break the bonds of civil law you only sever incompatible natures.

Miff and Viola were once more in their room. They rededicated the place with a kiss, and joyously did Viola meet the attack. It was to her the nectar that made the lifeblood thrill anew in her veins. Viola without God and without love was a brute, but Viola with love had the elements of divinity. Teach a woman not to pray and not to love, and you have destroyed the lights of her life and made bitter your own existence.

It is the painful duty of the writers to continue the narrative of Miff and Viola. We would lift them above vice, but we still see them there. We would make them good, but alas, they are bad. We would reform them, but their evil natures are still around us. We would take them away from dens of iniquity, but we glance in at the door and see them sip the beer. We would have them at church, but we cannot drag them away from the saloon. We hear men shrieking with laughter and see women lounging about in gilded palaces of sin, as though they were the happiest people in the world, as though the care and trouble of this life were nothing to them. It is the tremor of drink, the excitement of sin. The awakening comes hereafter.

In such places Miff and Viola are to be found. Arm in arm they enter the gin palace. The music begins; they seat themselves at a table.

"Hello, Miff; glad to see you out again," said a burly fellow.

"You're lookin' better than you did afore," said another.

"I will stand the drinks on your return," said a third.

"Here, waiter, bring the beer. Does your beauty drink?" said a fourth, looking at Viola.

"I am one of the boys," was her reply. A motley crowd gathered around the table and drank the foaming, bitter, obnoxious beer.

The curtain was rung up, and a girl, in an abbreviated costume, entered upon the stage; with a smile and a quirk she began to sing a coarse, rude song.

"That's splendid," said Viola.

The men applauded, and the prima donna, generally a prima dunce, sang another song. They applauded again, and she sang "In the Sweet Bye and Bye."

Tears glistened in many eyes. Viola was touched, and, placing her hand on Miff's arm, she said, "Wouldn't it be grand, if I could sing such songs as that?"

"I wouldn't like you to be up there. Those people on the stage are always bad, especially at such places as this."

"I don't care for that," replied Viola; "I am bad, too."

This remark seemed to please one of the men, and he took some liberties which she roughly resented, and Miff with flashing eyes bade him desist.

"You're a happy pair, you are. When did ye git out of jail last?"

"I was never in jail," answered Viola.

"Well, you ought to have been, anyhow," was the fellow's reply.

"See here, talk to me and not to the woman, who cannot resent your impudence."

"Yes, but I can, Miff. See here!" And with this Viola slapped him in the face.

The man was angered, and he raised his fist to strike her; but Miff was too quick, and the man was lying upon the floor stunned by a blow from his fist. "Good," said they all. Viola obtained some water and bathed the face of her wounded insulter, who, when he revived, arose and left the place without a word, but looked vengeance at Miff and Viola. His place was no sooner vacated than a youth of eighteen entered and sat down in their midst.

"He is a bird with feathers," whispered one.

"He is from the interior," said Miff.

A mutual understanding arose among them. Somehow they knew that the stranger was green. To an unpractised eye he looked like other men. Yet the men in the gin palace knew at sight that the newcomer could be easily duped. Was it his hands, his feet, his eye, his movements or conversation, that revealed his verdancy? Surely not the latter, for he had not spoken a word.

"Stranger, take a drink with us," said Miff.

"No, thank you; I never drink," was his courteous reply.

"Have a cigar, then?"

"No, sir; I don't smoke either."

"Will you play keerds?" asked another.

"No, thanks; I never play cards."

"Will you go to the green-room?"

"Where?"

"To the green-room."

"Where's that?"

"On the stage."

"No, sir; I only have a moment to stay."

"Well, stranger, it seems to me as though you enjoyed none of the comforts of this life," said Miff.

"I am quite comfortable, thank you."

"We don't want any of your thanks. Come, give us a treat, won't ye?" said a rather rough customer.

"Do," said Viola. And her eyes persuaded him.

"Order what you want, gentlemen," said the perfectly polite young man from the interior.

"Well, you understan' your business, you do," said Miff.

The crowd ordered the best in the house, stating that the gentleman would pay. "Here's to you." The glasses tipped in true Bohemian fashion, and the gentleman's health was drank with alacrity.

"Taste this, won't you?" And again Viola's eyes persuaded him. He took the delicately formed champagne glass, and drained its contents.

"I will, just for this night, see what there is of life, and I may as well stand in with the others. More champagne!" he called to the waiter, as the bottle was emptied.

"Two dollars," said the waiter.

George Dean paid the bill with a slight hesitation. He was poor, yet for once he thought he would pay for his experience. The champagne was again drunk to his health. The flattery of Viola, the compliments of the men, urged him on. Viola teased him upon his good looks, and Miff wanted to borrow a dollar; but George Dean had some sense remaining, yet when Viola touched his hand and said, "Please give me some money," he drew forth his hand from his pocket, and gave her double the sum Miff asked for.

Poor, misguided youth! Better for you, better for society, if you never had such experience. The fascinations of a low music hall should never charm a true man. You ought to despise yourself for ever entering one. No man is made better, wiser or more content by experiencing the dark side of life even for a night.

The men began to play cards. Soon the prima donna came upon the stage again, and by request sang "In the Sweet Bye and Bye" again.

"This can't be much worse than a Sunday school, if they sing such songs," thought George Dean. But alas, George Dean, before the sun makes crime hide itself for shame, you will wish you had never gone into the gin palace.

At last he was induced to bet on the cards, and Viola was the one who persuaded him. The poor boy bet on and on, until his last dollar was gone. His head was too hot to realize his loss. Viola was by his side urging him on, for Miff was gaining the money.

"This is better than stealing, isn't it?" she whispered to Miff.

It was midnight—the hour for crime and vengeance, the time when low saloons make money and criminals.

George Dean, in a fit of passion, struck a blow, and in return was assailed and brutally beaten. Viola tried to interfere, but she could not. It was she who bathed his head and bound up his wounds, and with Miff's aid she took him to their room, and made Miff put part of the money back into his pocket. They dosed him with brandy, and he slept under its influence.

In the morning Bona called to inquire about Miff. It had been two weeks since she had seen him. After his sickness he had avoided her; he would not look her in the face.

"Well, what have we here?" Bona said, as she noticed the youth upon the floor.

"He is asleep; don't wake him. He got hurt last night," said Viola.

" It seems to me as though you are rather unfortunate; Miff has just got well, and now you have another one on your hands. I am afraid Miff is getting morally worse, instead of better."

Miff did not reply. Bona placed her hand on the young man's forehead. His blue eyes opened.

" Where am I ?"

"Among friends, I guess," was Bona's reply.

And she looked upon his face and into his blue eyes, which shone so tenderly. She knew he was not one who was in the habit of being in such company as Miff and Viola. She looked at him again, and exclaimed:

" Why, it is Georgy. Those are his eyes and features." And she stooped over him and said, " Don't you know me?"

He shook his head, and then she said, " I am Bona."

"Are you Bona? Oh! I am so glad I have found you. I have looked everywhere for you," he said.

The reader must wait until the next chapter for explanation, for Bona turned and began scolding Miff. " I thought you were going to be good."

" I did try—I tried for your sake, but I can't be."

" Neither can I," reflected Viola. " We want to be just like you are. I can't read, write, or do anything. We must be bad, though we wish we were like you."

Miff had tried faithfully to be good. He had met the foe; but twenty years of bad training could not be overcome. You who would better humanity must remember that there is an eternal warfare between education and man—between society and the natural state. It begins with the first lisp "A, B, C," and the smoke of battle clears away only when we cross the line into the kingdom beyond.

CHAPTER XI.

"**He** who falls below the level, then rises above it, and maintains the altitude against all allurements, **is** infinitely better than the man who runs upon the level of common humanity."

George Dean was, years before, in the same Orphans' School in which Oswald Grayson had placed Bona. After years of separation, she remembered the bright face of **the** boy who had shared the sorrows of an orphans' home, under the direction **of** public patronage. **Bona** had escaped under cover of darkness, and wandered around until she had found her benefactress, **Mrs. Benton.** George Dean was taken from **the** school and placed upon a ranch by a man who was glad to get him for his board and clothing—a mild system of terminal slavery in vogue at most of our institutions for homeless children.

Bona was a sympathetic listener to George Dean's interesting **story.** We will let him **state it** himself.

"In the morning I awoke **and** found **you gone.** Everybody searched for you, and I remember seeing more than one cry; but the excitement had hardly subsided when I was called into the office, and was placed under the inspection of an old, gray-headed man, who spoke roughly to me, and wanted to know if I **was** smart. I told him I wasn't, and that seemed to satisfy him, **for he said he** would take me. That day I was taken from the place, and **was placed on** a **ranch** in the Sacramento Valley. Farmer Hoffman was a hard master, and he put me to work with the Chinamen **on** his ranch. I had to get up in the morning at six, and work until eight at night. I would never have had any education at all, but the teacher at the district school taught me some evenings, and I was thus permitted to acquire a little learning. I was bound to the man until I was eighteen years of age, and was compelled to work all the time for my board and clothes. From the time I was fifteen, I did a man's work. My hands are calloused, my muscles are large, my feet flattened by much walking. I did not live, I simply existed, and O Bona! often when sick and tired, your sweet face would inspire me, and I would wonder if I would ever see you again."

As he said this, Bona caressed him modestly. He paused, looked into her face; their eyes met—there was a blessed awakening. She realized that her girlhood was passed, and Dean felt the full force of the consciousness of young manhood. There is an affinity that exists between playmates that draws souls together in later years. George told his tale wondrously well. Bona wept as he recited the terrible hardships that old Farmer Hoffman made him endure. Her tears were sweet to him. Man would rather have woman cry at the recital of his sufferings than laugh at his awkwardness. George Dean continued his story:

"The last two years of my life were a continual fight against the oppressions of Hoffman. I was compelled to do work which the Chinamen refused to do. I ran away twice, but each time I was brought back and horsewhipped, and once was compelled to suffer from a whip in the hands of a Chinaman. Once I escaped, but I saw behind me a Chinaman in full pursuit. I was lame, and could not run very fast; still, I knew that if I reached the banks of the Sacramento, I could hide in the underbrush. On came the Chinaman, old Hoffman's trusted servant. He was a large, burly fellow, and was called the ' boss.' The race began in earnest; I could run faster than the Chinaman, but was lame. The Chinaman brandished a long lash, and came after me at full speed. If I reached the underbrush, I was safe, for I could hide easily. It was a mile, and through a grain-field; the wheat was about eight inches high, and the late rains had left the ground soft and in many places muddy. The Chinaman was close upon me; I grew pale with fear. He drew the lash and cut me around the legs. I stopped, grabbed a handful of **mud**, and threw it with almost irresistible force into his face. **He gave** a yell, and **before he could see I had** distanced my **heathen pursuer many rods. Maddened by the** defeat, the Chinaman again gained upon me. My **lameness became worse; 'I will reach** the woods,' I thought. The race now **became fierce, and fiercer; it was nip** and tuck. I could **have turned around and** fought **the** Chinaman, but **I knew he was armed, and even then,** I doubted if **I was equal in brute force** to him. **I grew hot; he gained upon me. The** perspiration rolled from my forehead. **The race** grew **desperate;** I was again tempted to throw mud **in** his face, but **the underbrush was near—I could** hear the **sweet** murmurings **of the Sacramento river.** With renewed effort I pushed forward. **At last I** was within the shade of the woods. I stumbled over a club; I picked it up, and, with an oath that startled **me,** because **I never swore** before, I **turned upon the** Chinaman. **To my** great surprise, he started on **a run. I became** the **pursuer, and** he the pursued. **I ran** him **into the woods; as he ran around a** small tree, I grabbed **his** pig-tail **and brought him to a sudden stop.** Then he started forward, but wound himself around the **tree, until** his pig-tail was wrapped several times around **and** his **head** fastened close **to** the tree. I stood there holding **the end** of **the** pig-tail, like a sailor holding a ship to her moorings, while **the** Chinaman yelled piteously, '*Yi Hi Yai Ha jidai Oi Yai!*' I tied **his greasy** pig-tail **to the tree, gave him a few lashes** with the **horsewhip and started off into the woods,** traveling day and night **until I arrived** in Solano County. **There I found work** with **a good,** honest rancher; he treated me **well and paid me good** wages, so that **I** saved enough **to take me to the** academy to **school.** This week I came to the city the first **time since I was** taken away, and alas, you know how in a moment of temptation I fell last night, but, thank Heaven, I'll never visit such a place again. I have had my curiosity satisfied; my lesson is learned, a bitter experience paid for, and I know that the little Bona, who cried for me when whipped at the orphans' school, will not despise me now."

"No, I am very sorry for you."

"You have not told me of your life since I saw you last."

"There is not much to tell. After leaving the orphans' school, I found Mrs. Benson, and you know my life could not be sad after that. I have assisted Mrs. Benson in her work; I pay almost daily visits to this part of town, and help distribute flowers and food among the destitute and helpless. You remember Mrs. Benson, my adopted mother, for I am Bona Benson. She still keeps her infant school, and hundreds of children are saved by her. She don't work by committees, like other charitable people, but does the work herself. I have nothing else to tell you, only that I have been very happy in my work, and that I see enough poverty and misery in one day, in this city, to keep me busy for years and years. Why, every time I visit Miff and Viola, they need help. They are both bad, but there are many much worse. I guess it was Miff who took your money last night."

"Yes, that's me," said Miff, coming forward, "and if you are a friend, stranger, of that girl, here is every dollar of your money back again, and I think if I should see Bona all the time, I would not be so bad."

"Don't Miff," exclaimed Viola.

"Why?" asked Miff.

"You know I am jealous of her, and when you talk that way it hurts me."

"Well, darling, you know I am not hankerin' after Bona's

style just now; you're a thousand times better than she is, for me."

Viola stopped whistling a low melody while she kissed him.

"Them two are in love," said Viola.

"You think so?" replied Miff.

"Yes; persons don't talk about nothing so long, unless they like each other."

"I wish we could get him out of this. He has all his money back; he ought to be satisfied now."

"I wish Bona would go. Why does she come here so much?"

"She must hate me now."

The quick ears of Bona caught every word they said. She arose from her position, and, going over to where they were standing, said:

"No, I do not hate you, Miff, but I pity you. I hope the day will come when you and Viola will cease your wicked ways and live to be an honored man and woman."

"O Bona, I would if I could, but I can't, and if I can't, how can I?"

"Get work; go away from here. Come to our Sunday school regularly, and leave Viola—"

"No; he will never leave me, and you are wicked to tell him to. If he leaves me, I'll drown myself in the bay."

"Well, if you love him, Viola, you ought to persuade him to be good, for if you don't the law will separate you, and iron bars will separate you."

"We are happy, as happy as you; nothing troubles us now. We have given your lover back his money, and cared for him; now take him and go."

"Don't be angry, Viola; Bona is our best friend," said Miff.

"It is no use, Bona; you had better leave us alone; perhaps we'll grow better some day."

As Viola mentioned the name of "lover," Bona blushed and turned her head away from George Dean.

"I will bid you good-by, Miff, and you too, Viola, but I know that you will change some day, won't you? Don't forget our meetings at the Children's Hall."

She then turned to George, and assisted him to rise.

"Where am I going, though?"

"With me."

"You know I cannot associate with you until I prove myself worthy of your confidence. Let me go away by myself, and when I am strong and pure, I will come back to you as a friend."

"No, come with me now. I have sympathy for you, and while I am sorry that you yielded to temptation, yet I remember that he who falls below the level, then rises above it and maintains the altitude against all allurements, is infinitely better than a man who runs upon the level of common humanity."

CHAPTER XII.

"There is a generosity born of greed, a charity overshadowed by sin, a giving that is petty larceny."

Georg3 D3an and Bona went away together. Miff and Viola were left alone.

"Well, we are rid of them," said Miff.

"Glad of it," replied Viola.

"I wish you were like Bona."

"I wish you would never see Bona again. Why do you always want me better than you? If I am as good as you, ain't I good enough? 'Tain't no use for me to be better than you. A woman oughtn't to be better than a man, anyhow, yet if she is bad it is awful, but if he is bad—why, it don't seem to make much difference?"

"Why, Viola, you are good enough for me—you are too good, you know you are. You are my flower, the perfume of my life. Didn't you steal pies, and bring them to me in jail? It was you who nursed me and saved me—yes, it is you who loves me, cares for me, and would do anything for me."

"I would die for you, Miff."

"And I—I will live for you, Viola."

"Oh, Miff, I am happy now. Don't you think I am as pretty as Bona?"

"What a funny question! Why, yes, Viola; you are prettier—only Bona looks to me like an angel, while you, you are like me. We are not fair and pure, as she is. Let us be that way. Let us wash our faces once a day, and get new clothes, and be nice. Do you know?—I believe the reason we steal so much is because we are so dirty. I never saw anybody steal that was real nice and clean."

"Don't you remember that stuck-up fellow? He was in jail when you were."

"Yes; but he robbed a bank. Of course such big thieves are always stylish. I mean honest men, who keep clean, never steal—that is, honest men like me."

"You are honest, ain't you? You gave Bona's fellow all his money back."

"I did that for sake of charity."

"Are you going to turn charity man?"

"Yes. Do you know what I will do first? I will give you five hundred dollars."

"I wish charity people were like you. But if you were a charity man, you would not give me even a flower."

"I would—I would send you to school. I would buy you fine dresses. I would give you something to eat every day."

"I am hungry now."

"I wish I was a charity man."

"They are not all bad. There is Dr. Halstead, and Grayson, and Bona—"

"Bona is not a charity man. She is a woman."

"She is better for that."

"Miff, let us do like the charity people. Suppose we go 'round and visit the sick to-day like they do, and have some experience."

"Would you like it?"

"Yes; just for the fun. We will go down along the water front to those tumble-down houses, and talk religion and such things."

"We ought to take some money and some food along."

"Get the basket, and we will steal some fruit, and perhaps there is some money in the drawer of mamma's saloon."

"It's a go."

"You get the money, and I'll get the food. We ought to have a Bible, too."

"But we can't read."

"I guess we are all the happier for that, because I always hear them talk about the dreadful things in the papers. Mam always told me there was lots of bad things I would never find out if I never learnt to read. She teached me grammar and spelling, but never readin'. Grammar is talkin', and you know I can talk."

"We ought to have a Bible. I can spell words out. Then it will look more like Grayson to carry a book"

They went down to a low saloon, and inquired for a Bible.

"Git you out! Vat you means?" exclaimed the irate man, with the proverbial nose.

They left, and tried at another place, where the German was much better than his business; for, when they inquired for a Bible, he said:

"That's right, my dears—bless you. It will do mit you good. Read it much."

Miff took the Bible, and when they got on the street they put their heads close together and began to spell. A puzzled look stole over Miff's face; he slowly spelled *Du sollest schanen Sie sich.* "Well, I never saw such queer letters before."

His English education was limited, his German was much more so. He gazed at the letters in amazement, and, picking up a piece of newspaper, he compared the two, and then, turning to Viola, said: "The blamed Chinese are making our Bibles, too. See, this isn't English," and he carefully pointed out the difference.

"It will do, anyhow," said Viola.

"Do you think I am going to patronize Chinese labor? No, sir." And he went back to the German, and threw down his Bible, swearing that he wouldn't patronize Chinese labor.

The next move was for the outfit. They separated. Viola, with her old stealth and cuteness, succeeded in getting a boy to steal an apple for five cents, and then gleefully watched the little thief pursued by the wronged fruit vendor, while Viola filled her basket with apples, pears and grapes, and then satisfied she waited until the fruit vendor returned out of breath, blowing like an exhausted race-horse. He received her condonement gratefully. She gave him a five cent piece, and walked away well satisfied with her work.

Miff was likewise fortunate. He entered the saloon, and demanded, according to his usual custom, and received his dollar. They met at their dingy quarters, and started out like people with plenty to eat and plenty to spare, he in his ragged coat and tattered pants, she in her faded calico dress. They looked generous—generous to wine; they looked charitable—charitable to sin; they looked philanthropic — philanthropic to every evil scheme. Thus these two, Miff and Viola—the street waif and the flower that grew and lost its perfume, crushed upon the cobble stone—started out on their mission of charity. Strange indeed the mission of the blacklegs, good work for petty thieves. Would that the hundreds who live upon the offal, saloon dives, dens, holes and worse than pits were engaged likewise.

They went down to the water front, in the narrow alleys where poverty and vice are boon companions, and the only struggle is for breathing space, where narrow streets and filthy alleys jostle each other. There are a hundred miserable hovels, and above all there looms a gloomy house, that frowns, like a sullen tyrant, frowning down upon a crowd of abject, poverty-stricken slaves. Sad, gloomy, desolate; decay and rottenness was apparent from roof to base. In one of the apartments of this house Miff and Viola sought an entrance. They knocked. The door was opened; a meek, gentle voice said, " Come in."

An old table, a few rickety chairs, that, like rebel soldiers, lost their legs in a bad cause, a tin candlestick, a rusty stove, with unjointed pipe, a wretched mattress piled up in a corner, as if ashamed to be seen without a bedstead, comprised the furniture.

"We come, my good woman," said Viola to a wan-looking woman, " to give charity. We're charity folks, ain't we, Miff?"

"That's our racket, dear woman; here's a dollar, and we will send the prayers around after a while. Viola has some food in her basket."

The children gathered around Miff and Viola, and looked up into their faces with their hollow eyes, and as they ate the fruit they were profuse in their thanks.

"You are the best charity people that ever visited us."

"You're awful good," said the oldest boy, as he devoured a large apple in double-quick time.

"Children," said the wan-eyed lady, " say ' Thank you.'"

"Thank you," said the children, in chorus.

"We only do our duty," replied the hypocritical Miff, as he placed his hand on a curly head, and stooped to kiss the lately washed cheeks.

"This is better than stealin', isn't it, Miff?"

"It's glorious to be charity folks. Let us make a business of it."

"I am sorry that we cannot do more for you," said Viola, turning to the wan-eyed woman.

"Why, you have done much more than any who have ever visited us before."

"I would read the Bible to you, but I cannot," dolefully exclaimed Miff.

"The Bible is a good book, but it does not supply food for my children, though it was the Bible that taught you to be kind and generous to me to-day."

"No, it wasn't," exclaimed Viola; "we learned this from Bona and Grayson."

"Perhaps they learned it from the Bible, because to be charitable is one of its most emphatic teachings."

"They didn't learn it at all; they were always that way—ever since they were born," said Miff.

"And were you always charitable?"

"No, mum; to-day we got charitable for the first time, but we will always be this way hereafter, won't we, Miff?"

"I rather guess so."

They had given all their food and money to the first woman, and so they prepared to leave. The wan-eyed woman said to the children: "Say 'Thank you' again."

"Thank you again," chorused the children, rudely.

Miff and Viola had no sooner left the place than the woman with wan eyes called the oldest boy to her side and said:

"Jim, run down and bring a pitcher of beer." Then she turned and chuckled: "Ha! ha! ain't they green charity folks, though! I wish all were like them. Sorry they hadn't a Bible! Ha! ha! I was mighty glad."

Miff and Viola went down the rickety stairs into the narrow street.

"Poor woman," said Viola; "she thinks we are awful good. Didn't we deceive her, ha, ha!"

"I feel cheerful after doing so much good. I am glad that we deceived her; she is very kind, and how well trained her children was."

They were again on the street. They had been generous—a generosity different from that of the man who paid two bits to a charitable object on the condition that the names of all those who subscribed should be published in the daily papers. He was generous, but there is a generosity born of greed—a charity overshadowed by a sin, a giving that is petty larceny.

The charity pair made a group. There are many groups upon the street. The old man and his aged bride, who for years have limped over our streets; the offal gatherer, whose life would adorn a tale; the urchin who steals to eat, and the youth who dresses to kill; the organ grinder and the addled-brained musician, who live by sound, harmoniously, if wedded to their fiddle instead of to one of Eve's daughters. The charity man—God bless him; may the sun ever shine upon him; and the charity woman, she is many. In her hands is a chisel; it has done noble work in our midst. Yes, the world is concentrated upon our streets; every grade and condition can be paraphrased from life, from the serf to the man of royal blood. How strange are the groupings we see, yet do not marvel at, in the kaleidoscope of life.

CHAPTER XIII.

"I saw a man lift tenderly the broken paw of a dog, and blow upon it like we do upon the injured finger of a child. A few moments afterwards I saw the same man push rudely aside the begging hand of a forsaken, poverty-stricken woman, and I said to myself, 'The instincts of that man are more brutish than divine.'"

Mrs. Benson was surprised when Bona appeared chaperoned by George Dean. Bona was her pet; of all the children whom Mrs. Benson had rescued from poverty and sin, Bona had grown up as her favorite. No one was higher, more kind, more beautiful than Renwood's daughter. Mrs. Benson pointed with pride to her, and often said, "She is worth a life's work."

When envious minds and selfish natures said that Mrs. Benson was a good woman, but taught erroneous doctrines, a good old church deacon said: "A woman who will train up such a child is orthodox enough for me."

"This is George Dean, who was with me in the Orphans' Home," said Bona.

Mrs. Benson received Mr. Dean graciously, and listened with interest to his long story of life upon the ranch, but he did not tell how Bona had played in love with him at the Orphans' Home, and how they still remembered the play; neither did Bona mention the company that she found him in. Bona often told Mrs. Benson of Miff and his strange conduct, and of Viola and her jealous rage. When she spoke of Miff, her tone would soften, and her voice, always smooth and sympathetic, seemed to be touched with a deeper pathos, and her soul to be filled with an undelivered message, until Mrs. Benson almost feared that the petty thief and reckless vagabond had won her daughter's heart. A new danger appeared, **for George Dean** held Bona's hand and talked of the past. Bona was happy; **her** nature was fresh, **like the** budding flower on a spring morning. She pitied **George Dean**, and he reciprocated that pity. Such pity is love. Two young hearts thus joined are inseparable. It is one of the attributes of human nature that a tale of woe will woo the truest and fairest maiden.

Bona knew nothing of selfishness. She was trained to give. **Her** life had been devoted to good **deeds**; Mrs. Benson had used her to carry out many of her missions of charity. Is it any wonder, then, that **she** first pitied, then loved George Dean? They had no vulgar courtship; to them **love came like** the fragrance of flowers; **it was not** studied, not sought, not purchased. They loved, **but they knew it not**; they were happy together, and they knew **not why**, neither **did** they inquire. Such love is pure, holy, sacred. **He** who **is** in love and can tell the reason why has studied **his** *bargain*.

Mrs. **Benson one day asked** Bona **whether she** loved George **Dean.** The question **was a** surprise; she **had** not thought of such a thing. In a moment **she** knew all; it was the awakening, the sudden unfolding **of the** budding flower. Her head dropped slowly towards her breast; the tears glistened on her eyelashes; the color of the rose overspread her cheeks in gentle confusion. **She** looked about, **as** if in search for George; then, raising her **head,** a new light shone in her eyes, as she said: "Is it wrong **that I should?**"

Mrs. Benson stooped and kissed **her, and** said: "I hope he **will make you** happy, very happy."

"It **is so strange** I hardly understand it all."

"You must both wait until you are older. I will secure him a good position in the city, and you can see each other as often as you like, and if **he** proves himself honest and true, you have **my consent,** but he must first be tried."

"I am sure he will." And then she thought of his temptation and yielding only a few days before, and fear came into her heart; yet she trusted with a woman's faith, and there is none greater.

"It is time to make your visits," said Mrs. Benson, and Bona once more set forth on her errand of mercy, like she did nearly ten years ago, when she first encountered Miff and Viola upon the street, and was forced to purchase her own flowers.

George Dean was starting to take his position in one of the wholesale establishments of the city. They walked down town together and parted on the corner of Montgomery and Market streets.

Bona, with her basket on her arm, proceeded toward Pacific street. As she turned an alley on Pacific street, she saw Miff, the charity man of the day before, teasing a Chinaman. Miff grabbed the Chinaman by the ear, and with the cruel propensity of a low nature pulled it until the Chinaman drew one leg up under his blouse and danced upon the other.

"Don't Miff!" And Bona laid her hand upon his shoulder. He turned, and looked abashed; then said, as a half-apology:

"He's only a Chinaman, anyhow."

"Yes; but he feels pain as well as you."

"I was good yesterday, Bona," said Miff, as if to excuse his action of to-day.

"I am glad to hear it; and what did you do that was good yesterday?" asked Bona.

"Viola and I did just as you do. We were charity folks; that's what we are going to do all the time."

"I am glad. I hope you will be real good, but you mustn't abuse the Chinamen. It is wrong even to despise them, much worse to injure them without excuse. It is wrong to hurt anything needlessly, even a worm."

" You are good, Bona; if Viola was like you, I would be good, too."

" **You ought to be good;** then Viola would likely be so, if **you were.**"

" **No, she** wouldn't; she wants to be like we are."

" Try."

" I can't; but oh! Bona, if you would love me! if you would live with me! fly with me! I would leave everything. We would go away, and I would be a man. Won't you, Bona? I love you, my life is yours. I—I'll kill myself if you don't—you must come with me. I'll never steal, I'll never drink, I'll never do nuthin' bad."

He grabbed her hands, **and** kneeling there in the unfrequented **alley, he looked** up imploringly into **her face.** A few women **gazed** upon the scene through broken panes of glass. The China-man stopped and looked back, and gave a satisfied chuckle, for **he** thought his tormentor had been conquered by a woman—man's most dreadful foe.

" I cannot leave you go; I love you!" And his **love passion** excited him until the bloodvessels marked blue streaks along their tortuous course, and then the intensity of his passion over-came him, and **he** lowered his head and wept the first tears that were not of pain, since he passed the innocence of youth, and **in** a subdued voice, **as if in pain,** he continued: " Ever since I met you on Montgomery street and stole **your flowers,** I have loved you, and for years I have been tempted to be good because you **were, and once** I didn't drink for two weeks, and almost went crazy; that's why I got hurt. I have dreamed of you. I cannot live without you."

" O Miff ! my Miff !" rang out upon **the street, and** Viola **rushed** past them, **her hair** streaming **behind** her **and** her countenance wild with excitement. " I am going to drown myself," she cried, and rushed down toward the bay. Miff left Bona, trembling with excitement, and started after Viola at full speed. It was only three squares to the bay. The street was deserted by all except a few drunken loungers and a lot of women. Viola had listened to the conversation between Miff and Bona until she could no longer withhold her outraged feelings. She then determined to carry out her threat to drown herself. She approached within sound of the surging waves. The billows moaned a requiem to the coming victim. A thousand voices cried out from the sea, "Come rest in my bosom." Behind her the cruel world, with its selfishness and sin, its crime and its coldness, hissed her on to destruction. Miff alone said "Come back," but she did not heed his invitation, but welcomed the music of the wild waves. She heard anew the splashing of the waters upon the wharf, and the seagulls hovered around.

Miff yelled again, "Viola, come back!" Like the flowers that wither at contact, she went on, as if to say, "Touch me not." She stood upon the wharf and looked upon the surging water. A wave came in, and as it beat against the bank it seemed to say above the noise, "Coward," and she heard the hideous laugh of the sea. She turned and saw Miff drawing near. With a disdainful sweep of the hand and an angry and forbidding countenance, she waved him back. With a despairing cry, "You called me a flower, then threw me into the sea," she threw herself into the bay, and the waters covered her in anger like the storm cloud covers the dome of the heavens. Miff rushed madly on, and, without thought of his own danger, plunged in after her. In a few minutes a crowd had gathered upon the bank, and saw Miff struggling in the water, with Viola dragging him down. After a desperate struggle he grasped a rope thrown out to him, and Miff and Viola were pulled on the wharf.

Viola was unconscious, and Miff stood trembling, waiting to

see her open her eyes again. In a short time she regained consciousness, and Miff knelt down by her side, and, in the presence of the coarse crowd, kissed his faded flower. It revived Viola and she sprang to her feet. Pointing up the street, she said: "Go; never look at me again; I hate you. Go to Bona; she is a lady, I'm not. I'll never speak to you again—no, not if you are dying."

Miff looked at her for pity, but she turned scornfully away, and started up the street towards home, the water dripping from her garments. Miff gazed with scorn upon the crowd of people, and then sullenly walked off. He had not gone far when he met Bona and Grayson. When he saw Bona, his head fell, and he could not raise his eyes to her face. "Miff," said Grayson, "I want you to come to my room."

"Well," muttered Miff.

Bona took Miff's hand in hers and looked at him, but somehow it did not seem to please him. That Viola had forsaken him, had tried to drown herself, weighed heavily upon his mind. He walked along in sullen silence, and was only aroused by a haggard old woman, who rushed at him and exclaimed, "You killed my daughter, did ye?"

Bona threw herself between them, and Grayson, taking the wretched woman by the arm, held her until a policeman came up. It was Mrs. Proctor.

Grayson muttered, "How low! and she was once a beautiful, innocent girl. She married an intemperate man, and, alas, she has ruined herself forever."

The two reached Grayson's house, where Miff and Viola had spent their first night together. When they were in the house, Bona went over to Miff, and said, "I have a strange surprise for you. Do you love me?"

Miff hung his head.

Bona repeated the question, and he said, half in anger, " I cannot forsake Viola."

" Don't you love me a little?" inquired Bona.

" Yes—oh, I don't know; let me go away—I hate everybody."

"I love you, Miff. Oh, Miff, you are my brother."

" Your brother—my sister! What do you mean?"

" Yes, I am your sister; that's why we love each other."

" Oh, Bona, my sister—my sister. I remember long ago that I had a sister, and you are my sister? I'll be good now, and Viola won't be jealous any more."

" Won't you kiss me, brother?"

Miff embraced his sister, then listened to Grayson's story of their lives. It was he who informed Bona of their relationship, and as he closed the recital of the story Miff and Bona were too happy to speak.

" Miff," he said, sternly, "you must now reform. Your nature is not wholly bad; your love for Viola, and your strange affection for Bona, which you did not know was a brother's love until to-day, have been the redeeming traits of your character. Your nature is bad, but it is better than some. I saw a man lift tenderly the broken paw of a dog and blow upon it, as we do upon the injured finger of a child. A few moments afterwards I saw the same man push rudely aside the begging hand of a forsaken, poverty-stricken woman, and I said to myself, ' The instincts of that man are more brutish than divine.' But your training has been worse than your nature. If you want to be, you can be good, but it will require of you a mighty effort—yea, a greater power than human will."

CHAPTER XIV.

" Here the story ends. Human misery continues, and from out the depths of humanity we hear the plaintive cry, "Help! help!"

Haggard and worn, Miff searched for Viola. Twelve months had passed since he had found a sister, and lost his love, Viola.

" I'll find her or die !" was Miff's passionate outburst in reply to Bona's appeal to give up the fruitless search.

Now and then Miff would hear of Viola in the saloons. Sometimes she was there only the day before, but she eluded his sight, or else the men were mistaken as to her identity.

"Alas," said Bona, " I'm afraid that Viola has destroyed herself."

" Then I will, too. I cannot live without her."

But Miff would not believe that Viola was dead. It seemed impossible to him. He did not know the power of the human will, and the loss of reason by conflicting emotions. Suicide, after all, is a natural relief to a frenzied soul. To die according to one's own choosing is sweet revenge upon the cruel fates.

Up in Barton alley, where Bona first saw the light of day, and felt the frown of a cold and heartless world upon her tender soul, Miff wandered, inquiring among his old haunts if Viola had been seen anywhere.

He paused before the very house in which he knew a mother's love. The alley had become deserted by all save the lowest of the low and the vilest of the vile. The wharf rats, the garbage pickers and the water-front thieves had their homes there. The houses were dilapidated; even Miff, accustomed to dwell in the slums, drew back at the picture of complete misery and desolation. He who had been so low wondered how human beings could thus exist.

There must be a vast difference in the very constitution of man. It would, indeed, be a grand economical principle in human nature if when man degraded himself to a certain line of demarcation, that he would cease to be a man, and exist in form and nature in keeping with his brutal instincts.

Miff looked a moment upon the place he once called home. The broken steps, the weather-beaten boards, the rain-washed windows, and upon the dirt that had accumulated in every corner.

"I'll go in," he said to himself. And he pushed open the door, without knocking, and paused, for the image of his mother and the dimpled face of his sister Bona came distinctly before him.

"Mother is gone now, and Bona is mine, good angel."

Thus it is that every sorrow has its complement in happiness.

"Hello! Wake up!" said Miff, as he shook a sleeping form lying upon a coverless bed in a back room. Slowly the form turned, and the eyes opened.

"Well, if it isn't you! I thought you were dead long ago."

It was Mrs. Proctor, bloated by drink and degraded past all human redemption.

The continual conflict that Miff had endured between his evil tendency and the efforts of the charitable people to reform him, had not been without its influence for his good.

"How low! This is the way of all who dissipate. Oh, if I should find Viola thus! But no; I will not think of it. Mrs. Proctor, wake up! Tell me of Viola! What a miserable creature you are! I often wondered what became of the thousands of bad women who go to the beer saloons and walk the streets at night. I know now. They end their miserable existence like you. I knew you when you were once gay, and now you are not fit to live among your kind, and exist here alone. But where is

Viola? Why have I lived all these years, and not noticed the final stages of our idle and degraded life? I'll love to my dying day the work of Bona and Grayson. Old woman, wake up! Tell me where Viola is."

Mrs. Proctor stirred and again opened her bloodshot eyes; but Miff could not rouse her from her drunken stupor, and left her. He was sick at heart. He returned to Mrs. Benson's in despair. The one object of his life was to find Viola. He could not believe her dead. "No, I'll find her and be happier than ever I have been. My life is hers."

Bona met him at the door, radiant in her beauty. It was her wedding eve. George Dean had redeemed his promise and proved himself worthy of Bona's trust. The orphan boy and the daughter of Jared Renwood united their fortunes, and their capital consisted in the hopes they had of a long and happy future. Miff had laid aside his street garb, and appeared in a fine black suit.

A great change had come over him in the past twelve months, since he had learned that Bona was his sister. Men and women on Pacific street hardly recognized the petty thief, the hoodlum who stole to eat, in the clean, respectable laborer, Mifflin Renwood, as he was called by his employers.

The change was wrought by love—the love of a sister and the love of those interested in the cause of humanity; and the cause comes from a power mightier than human will.

After the wedding, Bona pressed the hands of her husband and Miff in hers, and, kissing them both, said, "I have a brother, a husband, and there comes my mother," she exclaimed, as Mrs. Benson appeared, and a smile of much sweetness rested upon her lips.

"Bless you, my children, and may the generations to come be stronger on account of your strength and weakness. I feel it. I know it, that you will be grander and nobler in years to come than if in the past you had not experienced the dark side of life."

"Is Miff in the room?"

"Tell him to come to my place as soon as possible," said a messenger from Grayson.

*　　*　　*　　*　　*　　*　　*　　*

"You told me to come to you if I were ever in trouble, and I have come."

"Why, Viola, is this you?" and from the creature crouching upon the steps came a feeble answer, "Yes."

And from the folds of an old shawl appeared the smiling face of an infant as merry and as sweet as any cherub.

"I would never have come back, but Bona, my child, his child, must be taken care of, and I am dying."

Grayson kindly, tenderly, helped her into the house, and brought her some food.

"Now eat, and then tell me where you have been."

The eyes of Viola stared wildly, and a hectic flush was upon her face. Trouble and disease, misery and want had accomplished their life-sapping work.

"Tell me about Miff. Is he well? Has he reformed? Does he live with Bona? I named his child Bona after her."

"Miff has been hunting you everywhere. He is haggard and worn. I have been afraid he would drown himself in the bay, thinking that you had. He has reformed, and Bona was married to George Dean last night."

"O Miff! Miff!" exclaimed Viola, as she saw him in the room, and she could say no more.

Grayson procured some brandy and revived her.

"Don't kiss me!"—she waved him back—"Kiss your child!"

The child smiled, and the dimpled face was more dimpled as she held out her little one first towards him.

Miff looked at Grayson, and then the truth rushed upon him and peace filled his soul.

"Viola," he cried, "forgive me; Bona is my sister, the sister whom I lost. I love you more than ever I loved her. Forgive me, for I have suffered and have been miserable ever since."

"Bona your sister! and you love me, Miff?"

"I always have, Viola, ever since we spent our first night together in the cellar of this house."

"O Miff," exclaimed Viola, as she pressed his hand, "I wish I could live now."

"You will, you must live. I will not let you die. Live, and we will be happy."

"I wish I had come back long ago, but I could not. The ladies of the Relief Society found me crazy with grief upon the streets, and took me to their home and waited upon me, oh, so kindly, until baby was born, and then, after I had grown strong I left them and tried to earn my own living, but I could not, and sometimes even baby was hungry, and I was afraid to look for you for fear I would be jealous again. Then I named the baby Bona, and came here to Mr. Grayson. I know I am dying and I thought he would take care of Bona. But it is all changed now. Bona is your sister and you love me; I know when I am gone you will be good like Mr. Grayson, and will raise little Bona up to be a nice lady like your sister."

They watched a day and a night, and as the morning sun arose, warming the city and casting a glow over hill top, valley and city, the spirit of the flower went forth. The crushed, the bruised, the trampled-upon flower of the street withered, and the dew of love, which fell so freely upon the broken spirit, would never make the flower to bloom again. Oh, precious violet! if thou dost spring up in the street, why does not the Great Gardener transplant you within ivy covered walls? Thy life was a continual mockery against thy Creator, but alas, it was a human foot that trampled upon thee, and it was the decree of Divinity that even one flower, a pretty violet, should grow upon the street to be crushed by the wicked heel of careless man. Miff saw the cold and lifeless form and rebelled, but as he turned he beheld the merry eyes of the laughing child, and the great story of his life received his complement in happiness.

Here the story ends. Human misery continues, and from the depths of humanity comes the plaintive cry of "Help! help!"

Miff changed the name of his child to Viola, in honor of the mother he loved. On a quiet Sunday afternoon, Miff, accompanied by his child, with Bona and her husband, visited the graveyard and watered the violets growing on Viola's grave. If misfortune and poverty should come again to Miff, he would battle bravely, for the sake of the little girl he calls "her child." Tenderly and lovingly he speaks of the one buried 'neath the violets.

TWIN LIVES.

ANTE-SCRIPT.

The following story is given in almost the precise words in which it was related to us by a literary genius, an adherent of Democritus, with unusually long, silken white hair. He was a pleasant, shabby-genteel fellow of the old school. He wore a glossy black suit, threadbare at the edges, and a cone-shaped hat, with the outer rim a perfect circle. His cadaverous looks spoke for alms, but the melodious tones of a low-pitched voice told of wealth. Perhaps the man belonged to a planet world, and came hither to umpire the loves of humanity, the vices and virtues of men.

On a warm summer day, when the shadows in our office* diminished with the declining sun, he came in, as he was wont to do, silently, and then began the recital of a tale of marvelous friendship, the history of the tenderness of man's love for man, far surpassing the amorous and oftentimes selfish love of man for woman. We listened until the close. The narrator arose; his tall, skeleton-like form towered above us, as he noiselessly opened the door and went out. We have not seen him since; perhaps his monument, a plain and simple slab, is washed by the rain that falls upon Lone Mountain; yet he lives to us through the strange and touching story of the "Twin Lives."

THE AUTHORS.

' GOLDEN ERA.

Who was Adel?

A woman whose first memories were of California's glancing
waters, sloping hills, noble forest trees, rich grass meadows,
gabled houses, beautiful rivers and woodland dells. A woman
whose childhood went by like a fairy tale told by a soft voice on
a warm summer day.

Her lover said she was the loveliest woman that ever brightened a home. She had a face like the Cenci, a voice like an
Italian lark, a smile like a child, a grace like a flower's, eyes that
spoke without knowing why.

Such was her lover's description. Nobody wants the facts;
facts are hardly more amusing than mathematics, unless you can
whisper them.

Adel's life was without romance, until she had passed the age
of youthful fancies and girlhood dreams, and met Ralph Ather-
ton and Harold Eades, who stood before her with one motive
in life, their hands clasped.

In nature there are a million gorgeous hues and tints; yet the
pictures that are painted in sombre semi-tones, and have no pos-
itive color, are pronounced nearer to nature. A painter dare
not approach the real gold of the sunset or the yellow of the
sunflower. Adel has subdued tints in this story, for no one
would believe the life-likeness.

Ralph and Harold were like two mountain streams that attained strength in the solitude of the forest, and, meeting on the
meadow's level, flowed on together towards the great ocean of
the Beyond.

Ralph and Harold were friends; nothing on earth could separate them. They shared and shared alike the emoluments of
success and the bitterness of defeat. There were backward ed-
dies in their stream, but the current of their lives flowed irresistibly on.

After they met Adel for the first time, heard her sing and listened to the charm of her voice when speaking or interpreting the musical soul of some great master, they went to their quiet home enchanted with the new personality.

"She is beautiful," said Ralph.

"She is very interesting," replied Harold.

"Her songs are not like the songs of other women."

"I have listened to the songs of love, but she has not loved."

"She is full of idealities."

"She has strong passions, but they sleep."

"She has been used to her own way, and is indifferent; she has treated some men with friendship, none with tenderness."

"She seems cold; her life lacks the warmth of romance. She thinks affection ought to begin when the passion of its youth has departed."

"She has more mind and less frivolity than most of her sex."

"Yet withal she is a coquette."

"She dresses perfectly."

"She has eyes like the eyes of the boyish portrait of Shelley."

"Will you love her?" asked Ralph.

"Will you love her?" asked Harold.

"Will you or I?"

"Perhaps both," said Harold.

"Nothing shall come between us, not even a woman. We will not think of marriage just yet. Wait until we are forty, when maturity will strengthen our love, so that it may be divided. Be it as it will, nothing shall separate us."

And their hands clasped.

Thus they walked toward the moonlit city. It was an hour when the street was at its fullest and prettiest. The irregular blocks were half-lighted, half-dark; the painted and gilded signs swung in the shadows; the vendors were going home; half the places were closed and half were open; horses were trampling upon the streets; cars, with dim red and blue lights, shone far in the distance.

The inner life of these two young men was nothing less than a lofty soul-communion. The one felt the other's will before it was spoken, and from a distance came the spirit's call. The love of Harold and Ralph had an essence as tangible as the communion of saints and as lofty as the affinity of Goethe and as pure as the holiest spiritualism. These two lives were one, wedded together, not in the flesh, but in the spirit—a bond holier than matrimony, for no law can put it asunder. Twins by the natural affinity of souls, the key to each other's thoughts hung on one common hook.

Ralph was away for a week. When he returned a pained expression was upon his face. "I am losing you, Harold; you love Adel."

"No, no," replied Harold. "Come with me this evening, and see for yourself."

This time they called on Adel for a purpose. In a short time she was to leave the city, to return to the familiar scenes and faces of her home.

She welcomed Ralph's return so cordially that Harold was sure that Adel's manner to him was not favoritism, only friendship, half-disguised by unstudied coquetry.

Adel quietly asked Ralph many questions about his trip, and listened to his answers with such graceful interest that he was charmed with her silence, as he had often been delighted with her conversation.

Harold found others to interest and amuse him; yet, whenever chance offered, he was near Adel, and ready with a compliment.

"Why do you wear that red rose?" Harold asked abruptly.

"Vanity! It suits my complexion," Adel answered.

"That is an artistic idea. Your complexion is too beautiful to need ornament—"

"Or compliment."

"Truth is not compliment. I never use the language of compliment to you. You know that very well. It was our first compact, that you should believe whatever I say."

"Yes, I know," she answered; "but it is agreeable for gentlemen to tell pretty lies."

"Not, if they are not believed; but it is like you to doubt—it is like ten thousand other women, but I wanted you to be different from other women," he answered, half-bitterly.

He often thus tried to excite an emotion—a flush of anger or of joy. He wanted to test his power to please or displease. In anything save sentiment he succeeded, but in that she was immovable. She talked of love as though it were an incident of life.

"She is cold; her heart is tender, but she lacks the love passion," he told Ralph, when they reached the room.

"How lovely she was to-night," said Ralph; "not very beautiful, perhaps, except for her eyes, and a mouth smiling and glad with lovely curves to the lips, and hair dark as a raven's wing."

She never looked so well as when she sang; it sent warmth to her face. Singing, she looked like the ideal of Musset's poetic dream—singing love, bidding it come, yet unconscious of all.

"Are you convinced now," asked Harold, "that you are losing me?"

"It is friendship—wonderful friendship, dangerous friendship. Adel is honest, is candid, but her ways inspire love, as much so as if she sought it."

Happily for herself, she was so constituted that she could enjoy, with infinite zest, prosy things. She took so much trouble, she was so charmed with commonplaces, her smiles beamed so radiantly, her hands pressed **theirs so** cordially, her manners were so accentuated with the strongest welcome and eager enjoyment **of their** companionship that **a** man felt flattered at his own effect upon her, and he would leave her with a high opinion **of the lady whose** manners were so favorable to himself. Such **is** society. The art of **pleasing is** more based upon **the art of** seeming pleased than people think.

A day and a month passed, and Harold **left** the city to **seek a** purer atmosphere among the clear lakes of the **Sierras.** On his way he stopped at the home of Adel Stanton, and by her side he watched the noble, tawny sunsets and the sapphire blue of the skies, **and w is bathed** by the winds all fragrant with harvest blossoms, and **by the** sunlight in **which** the yellow tints of the hills flashed like **gold.**

He talked **to her of other** ones who had found **favor** in her sight. She listened and asked questions, and it flattered him. It **was** not vanity; a man cannot help being pleased when **one** woman shows herself interested in his position with another; **it is** recollection and anticipation combined. Then from the lakes **he wrote back** to Ralph the recollections of his pleasant visit.

MY **DEAR** RALPH: **You** almost drew me away **from Adel.** If either of us were to love her, something fierce in our natures would occur. We are vitally in earnest. Life **is** friendship, to us, and it is wonderful, passionate, pathetic, shaped by the gods of love and death. It would be better if we could laugh like Rabelais and smile like Montaigne; that is the way to take the world.

But I promised **to tell** you about **Adel. I** found her in **an** almost romantic home, surrounded by charming conceits, rich shadows and **a** depth of shade, where she is free to think, to dream and to study. An **in-**dulgent father, a kind mother and a sister growing like unto herself, **the** bent of whose mind is towar ls books. She finds the treasures of **scholar-**ship sweet; **she** seems led both by nature and habit to seek them.

I found Adel **in** the midst of a group of admirers. It is with supreme pleasure **that I** have discovered a fault in her; she has **a hasty** temper—not the bitter, sarcastic nature of a soured disposition. The dark cloud always appears as a storm; the calm afterwards, I venture, is tempered with a steady rain—of tears. And yes, I have found an error also, like a child or the calloused man. Let us think of her as a child in this. She cares not whence her life **came or** whither it drifts; it is enough for her that it *is*. In **her** own home she is more lovely than my poetic ideal.

With a tribute to this country, so that you may feel as I feel, I close. There is a breadth, a graciousness, a fresh and fragrant verdure in all this country not to be surpassed in charm; it is unworn and unspoilt, and although under its leafy woods the wheel of the gambler turns, and by its limpid streams and 'neath its **genial** sunshine the tired hypochondriac drinks, still there is much **of it that** neither gambler nor hypochondriac ever sees, and that is solitary **as the** highest peace and radiant with a brightness all its own. My descriptions are tedious. I miss you, Ralph.

Affectionately,

HAROLD.

Ralph waited **a few days, then answered:**

MY DEAR HAROLD: **I was pleased** with your description of **Adel's home.** You are beginning to discern; **you** will not be infatuated. **Our lives** will not **be** separated yet by a woman's **love.** That is right; woo the mountains and nature's grandest scenes. My nature can be in close sympathy with you in such a natural love. Woo the monarch of the forest; it will protect you from the storms of life—a woman **can** only cling to **you.** Let the breeze from the lake caress your fevered brow, and the ice-giant cool the approaching ardor of **a** passionate **love. I am** content to dwell awhile apart from you. At night my spirit meets your spirit half way between the lakes and the sea. Now I have something of interest to tell you. My spirit has gone straying 'neath the orange grove and found another spirit, as calm and sweet as the spirit of Adel. May it not entangle itself 'twixt yours and mine. I ask myself again, "When will this love life end?" Your spirit answers back, "Never!" Come back, Harold. I place the covers for you each night, and in the morning I fill your plate with the choicest the table affords. Come by way of the river valley, and we will meet at Adel's. Our friendship **grows.** We are far removed from the **practical business world.** Let us so **remain.**

Affectionately,

RALPH.

A week later Harold and Ralph were warmly greeted by Adel. Both were of an ideal and poetic temperament. They admired the same standard of beauty, adhered to the same principles, and lived in this for the higher life beyond. Harold was the the more impulsive, Ralph the more sincere. Harold was therefore quickly led to the verge of love, a fickle verge, that trembled over the abyss, as if to make him afraid.

Ralph and Adel sought the lawn. Harold stood in the midst of a family group and watched them. Adel looked to him like a realized fancy, whether shining in velvet and cloth of gold in a throne room or straying in a linen dress through starlit myrtles on Italian hills, or a California ideal, a kindred spirit, with eyes and hair to match his own.

They spent days with Adel, growing more intimate with each red, red rose, each fair lily, with its petals caressed by the sun, each shrub, each bush and each tree, until Adel and her friends became their friends. All this time no one could see any favoritism shown.

The impulsive and sanguine nature of Harold made him construe her cordiality to more than friendship; perhaps he was vain. He had no thought of proving faithless to his love for Ralph; it transcended the love of any man for woman.

Again they returned to their professional pursuits in the city, seeking fame, that which will win the applause of those to whom they would not care to bow. People who live in obscurity think that fame is a paradise. Those who live on the sale of their intellectual wares by popular caprice are seldom happy.

The world hugs itself to think it makes a woman debase herself to attain fame. It crushes and caresses between the rising and setting of the sun.

'Tis right to laugh at the cynic world when in tears and prayers over the sad poetry of Shelley, for the world dries its tears and telegraphs to the planet realms the story of his sin-cursed loves.

Harold's love grew more intense for Adel, yet he never confessed to himself or to Ralph the depth of his emotion. Then came a letter in answer to one of his own; it was brief, not a letter a maiden would write to her lover, but then Harold enjoyed the pleasures of hope.

DEAR FRIEND: I thank you for the flowers. I wore the red rose at the German last night. A year has passed since I left school, and it has been the happiest year of all my life—a year of continual pleasure and sunshine. You asked me in jest if I thought it possible for a man to love two persons equally well. I answer, in the same spirit, Yes, for I love four.

He read no further, but fell into a state of dreamy thought. The charm of love was upon him. He denied it again and again to Ralph when he was not accused. Yet he denied his love, and no one save himself would have ever learned its existence, had it not been for the news that unless he told his love boldly and immediately another would woo and win her. The struggle became intense to him.

He loved Adel.

The flowers were in bloom, yet it was not spring. The old year was just welcoming the new when Harold, forgetting the confidence due to Ralph, was again in the presence of Adel.

He waited for some sign; spoke words that would reveal his meaning; watched with anxious eye the influence of his presence. In her actions he saw encouragement; in her words he fathomed love.

Perhaps he was vain. He thought not of the future and dreamed not of the past. The immediate moment is the heaven alike to the lover and the child.

They were alone.

"I love you, Adel," was all he said.

He reached for her hand; it was cold. No difference what the answer might be, the heart said "No."

Then a great longing filled his soul to go to Ralph. He heard a whisper saying, "Come to me."

Harold waited for Adel's answer. It was frank and candid, like her nature; yet it cut like cold steel.

Harold went back to the city, knowing that he had not awakened the love that was deep in Adel's nature. His pride was not hurt. Like the transplanted oak, he was weak under the blast. The bitterest trial was yet to come, for though he firmly resolved never to attempt to win her, yet he knew that she unconsciously would always retain his truest love, save the perfect affection he held for Ralph.

He parted from her glad and triumphant, for his love satisfied him. Its complement was not missed. Like the romance of the rose: There was once a rose, even a rose, that had but one little, short life of a summer day to live through and to lose and perish, glad and triumphant in its prime, because it withered on the bosom of a marvelously beautiful woman and of a woman's kiss. You see, roses are as weak as men.

Ralph met Harold with glad surprise.

"I knew you would come," he said; "my spirit called you."

"I felt the call," replied Harold.

"I thought you were in trouble and doubt, and I went to our room. I took down your picture and knelt before it, and waited until I felt my spirit had reached you."

"Would that such friendship could exist between man and woman as there exists between man and man!" exclaimed Harold.

"What has happened?" asked Ralph.

"I love Adel," was the response.

"Then indeed you should be happy."

"But my love is dead already forever and aye, and is buried in the deepest recesses of my heart. My romance has been the romance of the rose."

"My friendship is sufficient for you, as yours is for me," exclaimed Ralph.

"May it prove to be so forever," replied Harold.

Their hands clasped.

Harold endured **one** life and dreamed another. He did not heed the disappointment, for it had no sharper sting than the **pangs of** a **song** bird dying in the summer's sere and yellow leaf. A **fierce** wrangle, that was all. Passion had made dupes of others—millions. Was he of shrewder stuff, to escape its meshes?

A man is not a man, if meditation, enriching the well-spring of the mind, does not, by **a** leaf in the future, reveal "the plighted hands softly locked in sweet, unsevered sleep."

Meanwhile the **lives** of Ralph and Harold grew more and more inseparable. **The** grand historic characters of David and Jonathan lived again, only Ralph and Harold had a spice of divine wickedness in their lives, which made them mere mortals.

The sun was low on a thousand hills, and Lone Mountain was wrapt in a shadowy shroud, and darkness silently crept from shaded hollows to the moonlit peaks. The low land of the Mission looked dusky and bronze-hued from the lurid glare **in** the sky. A purple cloud hung midway between earth and heaven, as if **to** keep away a little longer the rays of the moon from some sin-cursed spot in the city; far, far away was a glancing line that showed where the sun was sinking to the western sea to float its rays quickly to the red sands of Atlantic's eastern shore, ere the morning star tired of **its** day-break watch. And in the center of all **was** San Francisco, with the highest hill adorned with magnificent palaces, shadowed against the sea-touched sky, and all **the vast** cloud-world calm and serene, never angered to thunder, around it.

There is no view on **earth** like an after-sunset view from one of San Francisco's hills. Ralph and Harold admired it.

They entered a house where welcome awaited them, as friendly as the southern clime to the northern red-breast. Here their dual lives had the full luxury of expansion. An Italian song echoed through the house, as dulcet and charming as though it was Italy's own breath among the hills and along the shaded Tiber. Then came the plaintive notes of "Fond Dove," and Harold knew it was Adel before Ralph, with haste, had greeted the invisible singer.

Adel had surprised her friends with a glad surprise, for she had arrived in the city to make her permanent home in their midst. Ralph and Harold delighted to renew their attentions to her. The outside world said they were rivals. The world often hugs delusions, and individuals break forth in mocking laughter.

Yet it was not well with Ralph and Harold. That which before had been gay and joyous now became serious. The passion flower which Harold had ceased to moisten began to grow again, and Ralph became more and more attentive to Adel.

Harold at length was forced to ask, "Ralph, do you love her?" The answer was, "Have you ceased to love her?"

Then they remembered their first conversation, which ended, "Perhaps both."

Harold continued: "It will not do, Ralph; if you love her, I will go away—I cannot remain. We must part."

"If you were in my place, and loved her, what would you do?" asked Ralph.

"I would find out if she loved me, by asking her," answered Harold.

"But why do you not woo her? Why have you given up all hope?"

"Because I loved and she remained cold, cold as untouched marble in a quarry, and she is now pitiless, almost unkind. No, Ralph, the power to charm, to win love, is a magician's gift, a wand that wakes the sleeping senses, until a rose, touching the white neck, banishes peace from the bosom. The power to love is incarnate, and though the lover be faithless as the wind and rootless as the wind tossed flower, yet in him alone will she have faith. I want a love that loves me; if I must woo it, then I must keep up the mockery of courtship all my life. Love must be unsought by me, or else no life is worth living except my present one."

Harold stopped, agitated by his speech. Yet that same night he cast off a burden of dread, and, half-kneeling before Adel, exclaimed:

"I told you nearly a year ago that Ralph loved you. I tell you so again. We are rivals. My love is firmer, fonder than that of any one else. I tell you again, so that I may go away content. You have never loved. There is a sea of flame between us. When you have crossed the gulf, you will not look at me with the clear, candid, wondering eyes of yours. No; then you will only look back and wonder, after all, if my love at its depths was not too deep to be stirred by a pearl dropped on the surface. You will love some day like this, and my revenge will be, let the ghost of my love forever haunt you."

He stood by her, waited not for a reply, but touched her hand softly with his lips, as a bird's wing might brush an orange blossom in passing.

Harold returned to Ralph after the interview with Adel, full of vague feelings of unrest. Then for weeks Ralph and Adel were much in each other's society.

But Ralph was like a hunter out in the mountains. He is attracted by the plumage of the untamed birds, sailing away in the clarified air above the clouds, and lifts his rifle and sends death through the serene blue of the scarred heavens. The bird drops in the deep abyss, where no one sees it die. It is of no use to the hunter, yet he shoots the bird. And the bird dies.

Something of the hunter's feeling woke in Ralph. Perhaps he was false. Men who associate with ladies imitate their vices.

Now and then a thrill of savage jealousy filled the heart of Harold. Love has given to the Eastern and Western of the sons and daughters of men a mystical, silent sympathy that draws men and women together, as the sun draws the morning dew.

Adel seemed half-unconscious that a heart-problem was being solved, and that she was the result to be obtained. She had that kind of a nature which seems to unconsciously seek admiration; it came to her like the player's touch on a golden harp. She sought unwittingly only that which suited her own temperament; she gave the most careless disdain to the antipathetic. She was quick to anger; unbidden tears often flowed. She moved in a circle of her own; her world and her sympathies were belted by the sphere in which she moved. She was artless, innocent and inconsistent. She had the grace and manners of a fashionable woman, but not the frivolity. She went through life like the heroine of a southern novel moves through a story. She was as original as George Eliot's Dorothea, and twice as natural.

Ralph could always cast sweet trouble into a woman's soul; unconsciously he could arouse a nameless emotion. It seemed only natural that a girl should flush like a sun-kissed rose in his presence.

One summer evening Ralph and Adel were alone in a silent room, where they heard the beating of each other's heart. He came away happy, and, meeting Harold, asked him:

"Do you still love Adel?"

"Yes; and I will win her yet," Harold answered.

"Why—why, I thought—" and Ralph could say no more.

Harold knew the secret of his breast. Ralph had aimed at a

bird with beautiful plumage. He had crippled its wings, and wanted possession. He put his arm through Ralph's, and led him into the silent room.

"No, Ralph, I can never win Adel; but the time has come for you and me to separate a little while, and I will go away. By and by I will return, and then we will be happier than we ever were before. I will find some one who will respond to the magician's wand. God did not make this world so incomplete that I cannot find a flower that I can pluck without feeling the bitterness of the hidden thorn."

"I will go away, Harold; you must stay. I can go away without pain. You will win Adel. I will tell her of your wonderful love, and forget my own."

"But she loves you, Ralph, not me."

"I want you to win her," was Ralph's reply.

That was man's love for man. Harold went away. He saw Adel standing by the gate, dressed in a flowing robe of delicate pink, with a fascinator around her head that made her raven hair, dark hazel eyes and rich complexion seem more beautiful than art adorned nature. He ever afterwards remembered her as she appeared that morning, for, though often in her presence, he never saw her again.

As he went away, she said: "I hope you will meet your lovely fate."

"I hope," he replied, "that you will marry the man I want you to."

"Who?" she asked.

He thought of Ralph, but his love and selfishness made him answer, "Myself."

She turned away disappointed, and Harold remembered the look as the plaintive song of a bird that was dead. A few hours afterwards Ralph and Harold grasped hands, touched lips and parted.

A year and a summer day passed. Harold found enjoyment in the endless amusement of the world. Ralph's love remained hidden from Adel, like a culled flower between the pages of a poem. His love had a mystic charm; it was untold. Often he stole from the covetous night an hour to spend in her presence, and she did not rebuke the gentle theft. Those hours were sometimes perilously sweet.

One evening they were alone. She pinned a rose upon his coat, and he looked down into her luminous hazel eyes, and asked, in his own proud, careless way:

"Will you love me, Adel?"

"If you wish it," she whispered, with a whisper as low as the first breath of a distant sea.

Their lips touched. And he kissed her again. He was a noble, true-hearted lover, and rose above moonlight walks and nervous glances.

With glad expectancy, Harold was bidden to the wedding. He wrote from the mines of Chihuahua that he would come. The day approached. Ralph became uneasy. Harold did not come. Then came a longing to go to Harold. Twelve hours before the wedding, he became almost wild. He suffered intense pain; his eyes, arms and legs he declared were injured.

"Harold calls me," he said. "Something terrible has happened."

Every one tried to quiet and soothe him, but no avail. He declared: "I am going to Harold; the wedding must be postponed."

Adel readily consented that he should seek Harold, and with an affectionate farewell they parted.

Ralph was irresistibly convinced that some terrible calamity had befallen Harold. He took the first train for Chihuahua, in southern Arizona, and, thinking only of Harold, he sped onward towards his destination. He arrived in the mining camp, at midnight, and immediately made inquiries for Harold Eades.

"Poor fellow," said one of the Mexicans, "he lies in yonder adobe, dead."

The place was pointed out to Ralph, and, with the emotion of one standing over an open grave of a loved one, he approached the building. With staggering step he entered and knelt by the side of him and caressed his hair.

Then a feeble hand was raised to his face.

"It is you, Ralph. I called you; I knew you would come."

"Thank God, Harold, you yet live," exclaimed Ralph. "Yes, blind and crippled," he said, half-bitterly.

"If you had not come, I would have died."

"I am here, and will always care for you."

"How did you know I was hurt? I told them not to telegraph you until I was dead."

"I felt pain in my eyes and legs, just where you are hurt. Then, on last Tuesday at about three o'clock in the afternoon, I had a terrible shock,* a most peculiar sensation; it seemed as though an explosion had taken place under my feet."

"Was it not inconvenient for you to come so suddenly?" asked Harold.

"Yes, it was my wedding day. Adel and I were to be married just one hour after the departure of the train," replied Ralph.

"You did this for me—you left Adel on your wedding day for me! I will never be able to pay you for such boundless love. My eyes, oh, my eyes are gone. I am blind."

Ralph touched the bandaged eyes with his lips.

---

* This occurrence actually took place, and the eminent surgeon, Dr. L. C. Lane, was consulted and will vouch for its truth.

Such is man's love for man. Such is love without physical attraction; such is the love of the soul and the intellect.

For twelve long weeks Ralph staid in the adobe dwelling, caring for Harold like a mother cares for a child. Harold at length regained his strength, but at a fearful cost. He was blind, and had lost the use of one leg and his left arm. Of the after years he thought nothing. He only was happy—with his hand in Ralph's. Then, as Ralph led him away, he said:

> " Our bond is not the bond of man and wife.
> This good is in it, whatsoe'er of ill,
> It cannot be so easy broken."

"Your home shall always be with me," said Ralph.

"No," replied Harold; "Adel would not like to be troubled by my presence. I will go away to some private institution and live out my allotted time. All these things were planned before we were born."

" You misjudge Adel; she has a rare and noble nature, and will be glad to have you in our home."

There is something of divinity in human nature, after all.

* * * * * * * *

Five years afterward, Ralph is sitting by Harold's great arm chair, reading aloud the "Song of the Sea." From another room came a voice singing " Mary, call the cattle home." Adel followed the voice and stood on the other side of Harold. Ralph arose, extended his hand to his wife, Adel, over the head of Harold, and, drawing closer to each other, their lips touched. Harold smiled and asked:

" Five years, and not through courting yet?"

Bending down with exquisite grace, they each kissed a rose, and touched with it his sightless eyes. Then Ralph reached over that their lips might meet again, after his eyes **had roved** over her face in admiration. But Adel drew back **with a laugh as sweet** as that of the morning thrush.

The evening shadows creep over them and veil them from a too curious world. Above all there appears a pure, clear **and** joyful friendship—a friendship that never dies.

THE END.